"*O*hmigod, that's your guy! The one the psychic told you about!" Jenna whispered excitedly.

I shook my head fast. "No, he's not. It's just coincidence." I sounded breathless. My heart was pounding hard.

"But what are the odds—"

"Look, the psychic probably saw him at some point, and he stayed on her mind and when she was tapping into things, she tapped into her own memory, not my future."

That was the logical explanation, and I liked logical.

"He'd sure stay on my mind," Amber said. "He's totally hot."

RACHEL HAWTHORNE

Labor
of Love

HARPER TEEN
An Imprint of HarperCollins*Publishers*

HarperTeen is an imprint of
HarperCollins Publishers.
Labor of Love

www.harperteen.com

Library of Congress catalog card number: 2007930287
ISBN 978-0-06-136384-9

Typography by Andrea Vandergrift

First Edition

*For my dear friend Nancy Haddock
who dances on the beach . . .
and who told me about the red hat.
It changed everything.*

Chapter 1

"*I* see a spectacular sunrise."

An icy shiver skittered up my spine, and the fine hairs on the nape of my neck prickled. I know my reaction seemed a little extreme, but...

When Jenna, Amber, and I walked into the psychic's shop, we didn't tell her our names. So Saraphina had no way of knowing my name is Dawn Delaney.

Sunrise ... dawn? See what I mean? It was just a little too spooky. It didn't help that I thought I saw ghostly apparitions in the smoky spirals coming from the sharply scented incense that was smoldering around us.

Although I certainly didn't mind that the psychic considered me spectacular. If the sunrise she mentioned was really referring to me—and not the sun coming up over the Mississippi River. Her words were vague enough that they could apply to anything or nothing.

I'd never had a psychic reading before, so I wasn't quite sure how it all worked. I was excited about discovering what was going to happen, but also a little nervous. Did I really want to know what was in my future?

My hands rested on top of hers, our palms touching. Her eyes were closed. I figured that she was trying to channel whatever it was that psychics channeled. I'd expected the psychic to be hunched over and old—wrinkled, gray, maybe with warts. But Saraphina didn't look much older than we were. Her bright red hair was barely visible at the edges of her green turban. She wore a flowing green caftan and an assortment of bright, beaded necklaces. Her colorful bracelets jangled as she took a firmer grip on my hands and squeezed gently, almost massaging my fingers.

"I see a very messy place. Broken. Boards and shingles and . . . things hidden," Saraphina said in a soft, dreamy voice that seemed to float around us.

Okay, her words calmed my racing heart a little. We were in New Orleans, after all. I didn't need a psychic to tell me that areas of it were still messy, even a few years after some major hurricanes had left their marks.

"I hear hammering," she continued. "You're trying to rebuild something. But be careful with the tools. You might get distracted and hurt yourself—more than hitting your thumb with a hammer. You could get very badly hurt. And worse, you could hurt others."

Not exactly what I wanted to hear. I wasn't even sure if I truly believed in the ability to see into the future, but I was intrigued by the possibility.

If you knew the future, should you accept it or try to change it?

"Lots of people are around," she said. "It's hot and dirty. There's a guy . . . a red and white baseball cap. The cap has a logo on it. Chiefs. Kansas City Chiefs. I don't get a name, but he has a nice smile."

I released a breath I hadn't realized I was holding.

For Jenna, Saraphina had seen "fire that doesn't burn." The fire part sounded scary, but the not burning was just confusing. And that she saw her at a fair, or something equally mystifying. Jenna's brow was still furrowed, and I knew she was trying to figure it out. She didn't like unsolved mysteries. She couldn't pass a sudoku puzzle without stopping to fill in the empty boxes.

But a nice smile I could live with, as long as that was all he offered, because I was taking a summer sabbatical from guys.

Amber, skeptic that she is about all things supernatural, had tried to mess with Saraphina. She'd been the first one daring enough to ask for a reading. When Saraphina had touched Amber's palm, she'd said she saw color. We'd all been weirded out, amber being a color and all.

Then Amber had asked if she'd find love this summer. Since Saraphina's eyes were closed, Amber had winked at Jenna and me, because she has a boyfriend back home. She's been crazy in love with Chad ever since winter break when they first started going out. He's the first boyfriend she's ever had, and she's been a little obsessive about being with him as much as possible. Quite honestly, I was surprised that she'd come to New Orleans with us, leaving Chad back home in Texas. Glad, but surprised.

Saraphina had said, "Not this summer."

Amber had rolled her eyes and mouthed, "See, I told you. Bullsh—"

"But college . . . one better than you already have," Saraphina finished.

That had been just a little too *woooo-woooo* and had pretty much shut Amber up. Once Saraphina released her hands, Amber started gnawing on her thumbnail. And she was still at it. She had a habit of worrying about things and expecting the worst.

Now, it got really quiet, and Saraphina was so still that it was eerie. How could a person be that still? Was she in a trance?

Sitting on either side of me, Amber and Jenna didn't seem to be breathing. Neither was I. Was Saraphina seeing something horrible? Was she debating whether or not to tell me?

With a huge sigh, as though she'd just finished pushing a heavy boulder up a huge hill, Saraphina released my hands and opened her eyes. They'd creeped me out at first, because one was blue and one was brown. But once I got used to them, I realized they somehow belonged together—with her face. With her. It just seemed like a psychic kind of thing.

"I see nothing else," she said.

Although she didn't look old, she seemed ancient. I think she had what my grandmother refers to as "old soul eyes."

"Oh, okay," I said, wiping my damp palms on my shorts. "Thanks."

"My pleasure."

Maybe she was older than I thought, because she also sort of sounded like my grandmother.

"If you know something really awful is going to happen, you'd tell us, right?" Jenna asked.

Saraphina smiled. "I tell only what I see. I don't interpret it."

"Yeah, but a fire that doesn't burn. What

does that mean exactly?"

"I don't know."

"But it's the nature of fire to burn, so do you mean it's not actually burning or it's not burning me? See what I mean? It's kinda vague."

Saraphina shrugged, almost as if to say maybe we didn't really want to know anything else. And maybe we didn't.

I touched Jenna's shoulder. "Come on. We should go."

"But I need more—"

Amber and I had to practically drag her out of the shop, before Saraphina told her for the umpteenth time that there wasn't any more.

Once we were outside, the heat pressed down on us. Until that moment, I hadn't realized how cold I was. My fingers were like ice. I shivered again and rubbed my hands up and down my bare arms.

"Well, that was certainly . . . interesting," I said.

"Do you think she means Chad isn't my forever guy?" Amber asked. "Because I was thinking he was *it* for me. You know—my

7

first, my one, my only?"

"Don't get all freaked out," I said. "None of it means anything. Not really."

As we started walking down the street, I slipped on my sunglasses and adjusted my "Life Is Good" cap over my shoulder-length dark hair. The humidity and my hair weren't going to get along, but that was nothing new. After all, I lived near Houston, so humidity was a way of life.

I'd come totally prepared for New Orleans—also known as the Big Easy. I was wearing red shorts, sneakers, a white lacy tank, and lots of suntan lotion. My mom's parents are from Italy—the old country, as my grandma calls it—so I tend to tan easily, but I still take precautions. I'd known we'd be doing a lot of outdoor walking today because we had so much to see and do in the French Quarter.

"Then why'd we do it?" Jenna asked, looking back over her shoulder, as if she thought maybe something was going to jump out at us.

"We thought it would be fun, and we're in New Orleans," I reminded her. "Visiting a psychic is something you should do when you're here."

We'd arrived a few hours earlier, so we had some time to play today. But tomorrow we'd start working. Because, okay, the psychic was right. We were here to help with the rebuilding efforts. So again, she hit the nail on the head — pun intended — with the whole hammering thing. But it was also an easy guess. Lots of students were spending a portion of their summer here, helping with the many rebuilding projects in the city.

"She got our names right," Amber said.

"Color, sunrise, that could mean anything," I pointed out. "For Jenna she was totally off. Come on, a carnival?"

"She didn't say 'carnival,'" Jenna said. "She said 'fair.' Maybe she meant fair as in pale, not dark. My name in Cornish means 'pale, light.'"

"In Cornish?" Amber asked. "You mean, like in serving dishes? That doesn't make any sense."

I laughed, while Jenna rolled her eyes. Amber's comment was just what I needed to shake off the lingering willies. Sometimes she was a little out there.

"Look, y'all, it was something to do for fun. But there's not going to be a fire, Amber isn't going to break up with Chad, and there's definitely not going to be a guy with a red Chiefs cap in my life."

"You never know," Amber said.

"Trust me, I know. I'm taking time away from all things male."

"Why? Because of Drew?" Jenna asked.

"Why else?"

"You really have to get over what happened prom night," Jenna said.

She was right. I knew she was right. But still, it was hard.

Prom night was unforgettable. And that made it a huge problem. Because I totally wanted to forget it.

It was the night I caught my then-boyfriend making out with another girl in the backseat of his car. It had been almost midnight, the dance winding down. I'd gone to the restroom. When I came back to the dance area, I couldn't find him. I was going to text message him, but I realized that I'd left my phone on the front seat of his car.

A few minutes later, it was where I left my broken heart.

Wouldn't those make great lyrics for a country song?

"I'm over it," I said with determination, trying to convince myself as much as my friends. "Totally and completely. But I don't see the point in getting involved with anyone right now."

I'd put my heart on the line with Drew. He was fun to be around. He made me laugh.

He also had what I guessed you called star quality. He was in drama class, and he'd been given the lead in our school's production of *Beauty and the Beast*. He'd made a great beast because he has black hair but startling blue eyes. His performance had made me cry. He'd been so good! I'd been over the moon. My boyfriend had brought the audience to their feet for a standing ovation.

Now I wondered, probably unfairly, how

much of our relationship had been a performance.

The aromas of chocolate and warm sugar brought me back to the present. They wafted out of the bakery we were passing.

"Let's stop," Amber said. "Maybe a sugar rush will wipe out the worries about our future."

"I'm not worried," I stated.

"Yeah, well, I am."

It smelled even better inside—vanilla and cinnamon added to the aroma.

At one end, the long glass-encased counter had all sorts of pastries. At the other end were pralines, fudge, divinity, and an assortment of chocolates. Several people were in line ahead of us, so we had plenty of time to make a decision. And I needed it. I'm totally into sweet stuff.

"I think I'm going for the carrot cake," Jenna said. "It's healthy."

"How do you figure that?" Amber asked.

"Carrots."

Amber and I grinned. Jenna is a pseudo-health nut. Her dad owns a fitness center, her mother is a nutritionist, and her older brother is a personal trainer. But Jenna claims she's allergic to exercise. And when she's away from home, she eats every unhealthy thing she can find. Not that you can tell, because she's also on the swim team. She doesn't consider swimming exercise, just fun. Plus she's tall, so she has long arms that give her an advantage in the pool.

But her height gives her a disadvantage when it comes to guys. Jenna is slightly shorter than six feet tall, like an eighth of an inch shorter, which most people would probably just ignore, but she cares about the tiniest fractions because she really doesn't like her height. If someone asks her how tall she is, she'll say, "I'm five feet eleven and seven-eighths inches."

Me, I'd just say six feet.

Or at least I think I would. Having never been that tall, I can't say for sure, and like my dad is always saying, don't judge until you've walked in the other person's shoes. And I could never walk in Jenna's shoes because her feet are a lot bigger than mine.

She's taller than most of the guys at our school. Her mom keeps telling her not to worry about it so much—that boys grow into their height after high school. But get real. She wants a boyfriend now.

Because she spends so much time in the pool—with practice and competition—she keeps her blond hair cropped really short—a wash-and-fluff-dry style.

Amber, on the other hand, wears her dark brown hair in a layered chin-length bob. It never frizzes. She's also the shortest of our group. My dad calls her stocky—which I've never told her because it doesn't sound very flattering. Not that my dad meant to insult her or anything.

Amber's family has a ranch just outside of Houston, and she's used to hard work, which I guess helped her to develop muscles. She's really strong, which will come in handy over the next six weeks as we build a house.

"What can I get you?" the guy behind the counter asked. He was wearing a big smile, and I figured he was a summer employee, still new enough at the job to think it was fun.

My parents own a hamburger franchise,

and I've spent way too much time learning that the customer isn't always right and is usually a royal pain in the butt, but you have to act like you're glad they're buying your burger and not someone else's.

Since I know the truth about waiting on people, I always try to be a good customer.

"Chocolate éclair," I said, smiling.

"To go or to eat here?"

They had a small section nearby with a few tables. Sitting in air-conditioning for a while sounded like a great idea, so I said, "Here."

Jenna ordered her carrot cake, and Amber ordered a pound of pralines. Okay, so maybe working the ranch wasn't the only reason she was stocky.

"A pound?" Jenna asked.

Amber shrugged. "I'll have one here and take the rest back to the dorm, so we can snack later."

Our volunteer group was living in a college dorm, along with other volunteers. Our group is officially H⁴—Helping Hands Helping Humans. Or as its organizer, Ms. Wynder, calls it: H to the Fourth. Ms. Wynder thinks of everything in numbers. She is, after all, our math teacher. And it was her idea to bring several of us to New Orleans.

According to her, voluntourism—"people doing volunteer work while on their vacations"—is becoming increasingly popular. She'd even shown us an article about soap opera actors who'd spent time here, staying in a dorm like normal people and working during the day. Not that the possibility of running into celebrities had influenced my decision to come here—although, yes, I did plan to keep an eye out.

No, my coming here had more to do with putting distance between me and home. Getting away, far away, worked for me. I had no desire to run into my ex-boyfriend. I was hoping that before school started his family would move to Alaska or Siberia. Never seeing him again would totally work for me.

Nudging me, Amber whispered, "He has a really nice smile." She nodded at the guy behind the counter.

Okay, great. Amber, the skeptic, was suddenly a believer. I touched the brim of my white cap. "No hat."

I was a little taller than she was, and I wasn't at all stocky. I wasn't as tall or thin as Jenna, either. If we were in a fairy tale, I'd be the one who was just right—hey, it's my fairy tale.

"Maybe he just doesn't wear it when he's working," Amber said.

Maybe.

"Are you a Kansas City Chiefs fan?" Amber asked the guy as he set our order on the counter.

He scowled, as if he'd been insulted. "Are you kidding? Saints."

"Oh, right." She gave me a look that said, *What's his problem?*

His problem was probably that he was working and we weren't. I knew the feeling.

We ordered sweetened tea, paid for our order, and sat at a nearby table.

"Okay, so he wasn't the one," Amber said.

"There is no 'the one,'" I assured her, before sipping my tea. Nothing is better than sweetened tea on a hot day. I took a bite of my éclair. The filling was a combination of custard and cream, with a wicked amount of chocolate on top. Really good.

"Ohmigod!" Amber exclaimed, after taking her first bite of praline. "This is the best I've ever tasted. It just melted in my mouth."

"I think New Orleans is famous for its pralines," Jenna said.

"Its pralines, its music, its voodoo, its beads. We're going to have so much fun," I said.

"It'll be the best summer ever," Jenna admitted.

"Although I think you're wrong to swear off guys," Amber said. "It's like my dad is always saying: When you fall off the horse, the best thing to do is get back in the saddle."

I started shaking my head. We'd spent hours discussing the unfairness of it all. All I really wanted to do now was escape into summer.

"I think Amber's right," Jenna said. "Look, we're going to be here for six weeks. We're bound to meet guys, guys who are available. Why not hook up with one? Just for fun, just to have someone to do something with? Have a summer fling? Get Drew out of your system, completely and absolutely."

Why not? Because it was scary to think about liking someone new, knowing how much he could hurt me. I didn't know if I could do a casual relationship, if I could keep my heart from getting involved. I'd fallen for Drew really fast. And who could blame me? I mean, how many guys these days bring a girl flowers on their first date? And, okay, it was only three flowers, and I think he'd plucked them from my mom's garden, but still—the thought counted.

"Look, Drew was a jerk," Amber said. "Chad would never hurt me like that. And I don't care what the psychic said. He's the one. I totally love him."

"Because you totally love him, I should hook up with somebody?" Amber is one of my best friends and I love her, but sometimes I can't follow her thought process. Like the comment about the CorningWare.

"No, I'm just pointing out that not all guys are going to do something to hurt us."

"Just don't say absolutely not," Jenna said. "Keep yourself open to the possibility that you could hook up this summer—temporarily anyway."

"But we're not here to hook up. We're here on a mission."

"But I don't see why we can't combine guys and good works. I mean, think about it. Wouldn't it be the sweetest revenge, to post pictures of you with a hottie on my MySpace page? Drew would know you were totally over him."

"I don't care what he knows." Okay, a part of me still did. Yes, he was a jerk; yes, he'd broken my heart. But for a while he'd been everything. He was the one who sat with me in the hospital waiting room when my grandma was sick—even though my parents were there. He was the first one I called when I passed my driver's test. He was the one who got up at five in the morning to be first in line at the electronics store when their weekly shipment came in so he could give me a Wii for my birthday— because I wanted one so badly. Unfortunately I couldn't play it now without thinking of him, so I'd stopped using it. Drew and I did so much together, he was a part of so many things that the memories formed a web, connecting every-thing and making me feel trapped.

"I'm not hooking up with anyone. That's final," I said.

Jenna shrugged. "Fine. Don't. But I plan to." Having finished her carrot cake, she reached into the box and took out a praline. "I mean, I've never even had a date."

"The guys at school are so stupid," Amber said.

Jenna smiled. "I guess."

"I think you both should get boyfriends while we're here," Amber said.

How many times did I have to say no?

"If we did, you'd be hanging out alone," I felt compelled to point out.

"Don't worry about me," Amber said. "I'll always find someone to hang with. As my dad says, I've never met a stranger."

"I've got a crazy idea." Jenna leaned forward, her blue eyes twinkling. "We should go to a voodoo shop and have a hex put on Drew and get a love potion for me."

"No thanks. I'm still freaked out about the

psychic reading," Amber said. "I'm not sure if I'm ready for voodoo rituals."

The bakery door opened and three guys wearing sunglasses sauntered in. They looked a little older than us. College guys, probably. It looked like they hadn't shaved in a couple of days. Scruffy—but in a sexy kind of way.

They were wearing cargo shorts, Birkenstocks, and wrinkled T-shirts. They grinned at us as they walked by our table. The one in the middle had a really, really nice smile.

He was also wearing a red cap.

A red cap with a Kansas City Chiefs logo on it.

Chapter 2

"*O*hmigod, that's your guy!" Jenna whispered excitedly.

It couldn't be. It just couldn't be.

I was trying not to hyperventilate, trying not to lose it. There were probably a hundred guys in the city wearing that hat. Maybe a Kansas City Chiefs' fanatics convention was going on. Or a preseason game. Was it time for preseason games yet?

I shook my head fast. "No, he's not."

Amber leaned across the table and said in a low voice, "Is anyone else totally freaking out here?"

"Don't you think he's her guy?" Jenna asked.

"Well, yeah! Absolutely."

23

"It's just coincidence." I sounded breathless. My heart was pounding hard.

"I'd buy into that if he was wearing a Saints hat. But Kansas City? Why would he be wearing that?" Jenna asked.

"Maybe he's from Kansas City."

"But what are the odds—"

"Look, people visit here from all over. Saraphina probably saw him at some point, and he stayed on her mind and when she was tapping into things, she tapped into her own memory, not my future."

That was the logical explanation, and I liked logical.

"He'd sure stay on my mind," Amber said. "He's totally hot."

Her brown eyes widened. "Oh gosh, don't tell Chad I noticed another guy. He would so not understand."

"You don't think guys with girlfriends notice other girls?" Jenna asked.

"Once you're with someone, that should be your focus," Amber said, but she didn't sound as though she was totally convinced—and she was still eyeing the guys at the counter, with almost as much interest as she had for the pralines.

"My brother says even though he's ordered the entrée, he can still look over the menu," Jenna said.

Her brother—the personal trainer—was five or six years older than she was and living with his girlfriend. If a guy was living with me, I would *not* want him still looking over the menu.

"Yeah, well, sometimes that can make you change your order. Just ask Drew," I said.

"I guess, but still it seems a shame not to be able to look at all," Jenna said. "And I'm crushing on actors all the time. Does that count?"

She'd developed a thing for Nick Simmons. It didn't hurt that he was six feet seven inches tall. She had every episode of *Gene Simmons: Family Jewels* still saved on her TiVo.

"That's just fantasy," I said.

And I didn't want to admit it, but the guys who'd just walked in were sort of fantasy, too. I mean, I couldn't see a college guy really being interested in me, and these three were definitely not in high school. They seemed too confident, cocky almost, but not conceited. Hard to describe.

I looked toward the counter. With one smooth motion, Red Cap removed his sunglasses. Our eyes met. From this distance, I couldn't tell the color, but they looked dark. He smiled. He really did have an inviting smile—a smile that promised fun and maybe . . . more. As though suddenly embarrassed, or maybe he was shy, or not impressed with me, he turned away and said something to one of his friends. The guy he was talking to was amazingly tall.

"How tall do you think that other guy is?" Jenna asked.

"Which one specifically?" I asked.

She glowered, because I was giving her a hard time. It was obvious which one she was referring to.

"Over six feet. Easy," I said. "Maybe close to six six."

I could hear the guys talking in hushed tones, not what they were saying, but I was pretty sure they weren't discussing the pastry options. Maybe I'd picked up some of Saraphina's psychic abilities.

"I think we should probably go," I said.

"Why?" Jenna asked. "We're not on a schedule."

She was making eye contact with the tall guy. He'd removed his sunglasses, and his eyes were definitely a light color, blue or green.

"Stop that," I whispered. "What if they come over?"

"What if they do?"

Okay, this was embarrassing to admit because I had at one time, after all, had a boyfriend, but the truth is, I didn't have a lot of experience flirting. Drew and I got together pretty soon after Mom gave me permission to start dating, and you don't flirt with your boyfriend. I mean, I never flirted with Drew.

I was tutoring him in math after school— part of a program sponsored by the National Honor Society—when he said he was having trouble with a really complicated formula. Then he wrote out Dawn + Drew = x.

He'd looked at me with those gorgeous blue

27

eyes of his and asked, "Could x equal date?"

And yep, as corny as it was, I'd fallen for it. Totally. That was the middle of my sophomore year, and we'd been together until our junior prom when I'd realized the answer wasn't an absolute constant—that the equation contained hidden variables.

"Look, I'm really not ready to deal with this." I shoved back my chair and stood.

Jenna rolled her eyes and did the same, while Amber closed up her praline box.

"Whoa! You're tall." Tall Guy had walked over and was smiling at Jenna.

Jenna smiled. It was the first time she didn't seem embarrassed by her height. I had a feeling if he asked how tall she was, she'd tell him six feet. No problem.

"So are you," she said.

Tall Guy shot an air ball at an imaginary hoop just over Jenna's head.

"You play basketball?" Jenna asked.

He nodded. "You?"

"Swim team."

He grinned really broadly. Nice smile. Really

nice smile. Maybe all guys had nice smiles, and Saraphina's prediction meant nothing.

"I like those uniforms better," he said. "A whole lot better."

"They're not uniforms. They're swimsuits."

He just winked at her, and I could see her cheeks turning red.

The guy behind the counter, oblivious to the flirting going on, rapped his knuckles on the glass case. "Hey, big guy, you want something or not?"

I sort of expected Tall Guy to point at Jenna and say, "Yeah, I want her."

But he didn't.

All three guys turned their attention to the clerk.

I could tell Jenna was disappointed that the flirting session had so easily and swiftly come to an end. With her cheeks turning even redder, she headed toward the door. Amber and I hurried to catch up.

"See ya!" Tall Guy called out.

Smiling, Jenna looked back over her shoulder and waved. Once we were outside, she said,

"Was he interested or not?"

"I think boys always choose food over girls," Amber said. "It's a caveman mentality of survival."

"Do you even know what you're talking about?" Jenna asked.

"Not really, but it was getting a little intense in there."

"I thought you were okay with Dawn and me hooking up with someone, that you never met a stranger?"

"I am okay with it; I just wasn't ready for it to happen five minutes after we started talking about it."

"So maybe we should have stayed."

"But we were finished eating," I pointed out.

"So? Would it have been a bad thing to be obvious that *I* was interested?"

"Do you want to go back in?" I asked. "Because if you really want to—"

Jenna shook her head. "Nah, no reason to go back in now. It would make us look fickle or something. Maybe desperate. Besides, it'd just be a one-night thing, and we're supposed to be in front of the gate to Jackson Square at eleven tonight so Ms. Wynder can pick us up. Not sure I want to admit I have a curfew to an older guy. But he was certainly tall."

"And cute," Amber said.

"The curfew isn't really a curfew. I mean, Ms. Wynder is providing transportation, because we don't have a car," I said.

"She's responsible for us. Chaperone. Sort of," Amber said.

There were three other volunteers, six of us in all. Because Ms. Wynder had organized our group, she'd promised to look out for us, but it wasn't a school trip and no one had signed any binding contracts, consent forms, or legal documents. She'd driven us here in her minivan and arranged for us to stay in the dorm. She'd provided transportation to the French Quarter with the promise to pick us up later and the warning to not get into any trouble. Although I wasn't exactly sure what she'd do if we did get into trouble. Call our parents, I guessed.

But was she really a chaperone? If she was, wouldn't she have stayed with us, kept an eye on us, instead of cutting us loose to find our own entertainment? Although to be honest, I was glad she hadn't tagged along. I think she's, like, thirty.

"You girls are going to be seniors in the fall. I trust you to be responsible," she'd said when she dropped us off.

Telling us she trusted us was tricky on her part, because it made us feel like we had to behave. Not that we were known for getting into trouble or walking around with fake IDs, but still. Away from home, parents, and anyone who knew us . . .

I think we'd planned to do a little misbehaving.

I thought of the inviting smile in the bakery. I was probably crazy to have walked away. Why was it so scary now to even think about getting together with a guy?

I hated Drew. He made me question everything.

"So what *are* we gonna do tonight?" Jenna asked as we crossed the street after a horse and carriage rattled by.

I almost said that I wanted to ride in a carriage, but it seemed like such a touristy thing to do. Of course, we were tourists, so I supposed it would be okay.

Pointing to a door where a sign proclaimed TAROT CARD READINGS, Amber said, "Maybe we should pop in there. You know, verify what the psychic told us."

"Or maybe we should have our palms read," Jenna suggested. "See if Tall, Dark, and Handsome back there is in my future."

"If he was, don't you think Saraphina would have said something?" I asked.

"I guess there's no way to interpret 'fire that doesn't burn' as applying to him," Jenna said.

"Maybe if he had red hair," Amber suggested.

But his hair had been dark, buzzed short.

"Could 'fire that doesn't burn' mean passion that doesn't happen?" Jenna asked.

I was totally confused.

"What?" Amber asked, obviously confused, too.

"Maybe there would have been passion between us, but I walked away."

Actually, I thought, that sort of made sense.

"If that's the case, then you were supposed to walk away," I said.

"So why predict it? So I live with regret?"

"Who knows? I bet people go insane after a reading, trying to interpret what everything means," I said.

Jenna laughed. "I am obsessing, but you know me and puzzles. I'll stop thinking about it now."

"Sure you don't want to have a tarot reading?" Amber asked.

"I'm sure. Let's just walk around. We've got six weeks to explore things, and I'm not really sure I want the future confirmed. I mean, in theory, it sounds like a good idea, but it's just not nearly as reassuring as I thought it would be."

The French Quarter had been spared most of the devastation that had hit the other areas of New Orleans. There wasn't much traffic, other than foot traffic. I think it was because the streets were so narrow that cars barely missed swiping other passing cars and everyone had to drive so slowly. I wouldn't want to drive here.

Better to park at the outskirts and walk or catch a streetcar.

The buildings revealed interesting architecture, kind of romantic. A lot of brick with wrought-iron balconies decorated with flowers. It reminded me of the Lestat vampire novels. I was a huge Anne Rice fan. Before the summer was over, I wanted to see her house in the Garden District. I could imagine vampires walking these streets. And we hadn't even been here at night yet.

By the time we hit Decatur Street, the sun had dropped behind the buildings and dusk was settling in. We were really hungry, our afternoon snack a couple of hours behind us. Even finishing off Amber's pralines while we'd explored various avenues and shops hadn't ruined our appetite.

"Hey, Bubba Gump Shrimp Company," Amber said, pointing to a restaurant. "I love the Forrest Gump movie. Let's eat there."

"Works for me," I said.

We walked inside. To the right was a bar area and to the left was a gift shop with all sorts of Bubba Gump restaurant and Forrest Gump souvenirs. RUN, FORREST, RUN signs. DVDs of the movie. A suit that Tom Hanks had worn in the movie was on display.

"Three?" the hostess asked.

"Yeah," Jenna said.

"Please come with me."

We followed her through the crowded restaurant to the back and up a set of stairs into a smaller dining area. Booths rested along the wall and tables were in the center. We were the only ones sitting up there.

"Wherever you want," the hostess said.

We took a square table near the window, with Jenna and me sitting on either side of Amber.

"The server will be up in a minute. Enjoy." The hostess walked out of the room.

"Do we stink or something?" Jenna asked as she opened the menu. "That we have to be isolated from the other customers?"

"Well, we have been walking around most of the afternoon," Amber said.

"Still."

"I like being up here," I said. "It's quiet, and

we can hear ourselves talk. It seemed kind of noisy downstairs."

"It was noisy because people were down there. Maybe we'd see something interesting."

"Are you saying we're not interesting?" I teased.

"We're away from home. It just seems like we should meet other people, experience things."

"You're still thinking about that tall guy," I guessed.

"Yeah. Missed opportunity." Jenna sighed. "So, okay, I'm fine now. I've vented. What are y'all gonna order?"

That was the thing about Jenna. She never stayed angry, never held grudges. She probably would have even forgiven her boyfriend if he had ruined her prom night. I was discovering that I held a grudge awhile longer. I wasn't certain if it was an aspect of my personality that I really liked, but at the same time, I thought being too forgiving could be a fault, too.

I just really didn't understand where I went wrong with Drew. We'd always gotten along. We'd never fought. We'd never gotten on each other's nerves. I'd thought he was the one . . . until he wasn't.

"Well, duh?" Amber said. "Shrimp. We have to order shrimp. Boiled shrimp, fried shrimp, sautéed shrimp, shrimp scampi, shrimp cocktail, butterfly shrimp—"

I laughed. "Enough already. We get it."

We heard the footsteps echoing on the stairs.

"I think we're about to have company," Jenna said.

"Unless our server is an alien with multiple legs," I teased.

"Very funny."

"Well, at least putting us up here wasn't personal," Amber said.

The hostess walked into the room, three guys following behind her.

"Hey, we know them!" the tallest guy said.

Amber gasped. I felt my mouth drop open. Jenna's eyes widened.

They were the guys from the bakery.

Chapter 3

What were the odds? That with all the different restaurants in New Orleans, they'd pick the same one as us?

Astronomical.

The hostess told them the same thing she told us, to sit anywhere they wanted, and I halfway expected them to say they wanted to sit with us. They didn't. They took a table at the far end of the room. Once they started talking, we could hear only a low rumble.

"Bummer," Jenna said under her breath. "I thought maybe they'd ask to sit with us. Maybe we should—"

"Are you ready to order?"

The server stood there, and I hadn't even

seen him come in. I'd been paying too much attention to Red Cap and trying not to freak out. Maybe they were stalkers. Maybe they'd been following us all along and we'd been too distracted looking at petunias on balconies to notice.

"Who wants to go first?" the server prodded, obviously in a hurry. He crouched down, put his pad on the table, and started tapping his pencil impatiently against the pad.

We each ordered fried shrimp. When the waiter walked over to the guys' table to get their order, Jenna leaned in. "What do you think it means?" she asked.

"What?" I asked.

She rolled her eyes to the side, toward the guys. "That they're here."

"Either they like seafood or they're huge fans of *Forrest Gump*."

"I think it's a sign," Amber said. "We should have done a tarot reading. Then we'd know for sure."

"You don't even believe in stuff like that," I reminded her.

"Maybe I'm starting to believe. You have to

admit that Saraphina got more things right than she got wrong. I mean, really—did she get anything wrong?"

I wasn't exactly sure how we could judge that. We were assuming a lot of things . . . like this Red Cap was my Red Cap. Maybe he wasn't.

I jumped when I heard a chair scrape across the floor. I'm not usually easily spooked. Nerves of steel, like Superman. But, okay, maybe I was just a little unsettled by how our day was going.

I looked over. The server had left. The guys walked to our table.

"We were wondering," Tall Guy said, looking at Jenna as he spoke, "do you know how much a polar bear weighs?"

Jenna looked at us, looked back at him. "No."

"Enough to break the ice." He grinned, and Jenna grinned back at him.

The other two guys were shaking their heads.

"Seriously," Tall Guy said. "We were talking. We're new to town, don't know anyone, and fate seems to be working here. Three of you, three of us. Running into one another again. What can I say? It seems like destiny."

Did he really say destiny?

"So what say we share a table," he suggested.

"Okay," Jenna said, nodding so rapidly that her head was almost a blur.

The guys moved a chair out of the way, then shoved the closest table against the empty side of ours. Without hesitation, Tall Guy sat next to Jenna. No surprise there. Red Cap and the remaining guy exchanged glances. Finally Red Cap sat next to me, which left Amber sitting across from the third guy.

"I'm Tank," Tall Guy said.

Jenna released a laugh, then slapped her hand over her mouth. "Sorry. It's not a funny name. It's just, were you—are you—in the military or something?"

"Nah, not even close. It's just a nickname, better than Theodore."

Her eyes widened. "Your parents named you Theodore?"

"Yeah, what were they thinking, right? Family tradition. You gotta hate 'em, though."

He pointed to Red Cap. "That's Brady. And Sean."

Jenna introduced our group.

Looking at me, Brady touched the brim of his cap. "Like your hat."

"Like yours, too."

"I thought I noticed you looking at it earlier. You a Chiefs fan?"

I shook my head. "Texans." I wasn't really into football, but I believed in hometown loyalty.

"You from Houston?"

"Yeah. Well, actually, Katy, but most people don't know where—"

"We know where Katy is. We go to Rice."

Okay, so they *were* college guys. Rice University is in Houston, and Katy is about thirty minutes west of Houston.

"Talk about your small world," Brady said, smiling.

"Yeah, really."

He looked past me to Amber. "You know, we should change seats. That way you can talk to Sean."

Amber looked startled, probably because Brady had already stood up.

"Oh, yeah, sure, okay, yeah."

Brady dropped into the chair that Amber vacated. Jenna didn't even seem to notice that she had a different person sitting on the other side of her. She and Tank were talking really quietly, with hushed voices. It was strange seeing Jenna with a guy who seemed totally into her. I mean, I'd never understood guys not giving her attention, but still . . .

"So, you're from Katy," Brady said, drawing my attention back to him.

"Yeah," I said. Did he ever stop smiling? And why did it irritate me? Because I didn't want to like him. This summer wasn't about hooking up with someone. It was about doing good works.

Although I had to admit I was flattered that he was showing interest.

"Where do you go to college?"

I released a self-conscious laugh. "Actually we're high school juniors . . . or we were. We'll be seniors in the fall. I'm never sure what to call myself during the summer. You know? Am I what I was, or what I'm going to be?"

Why was I going on and on about nothing? That wasn't like me. But then, what was these days?

His smile grew. I wanted to reach out and touch the corner of his mouth. Strange, really strange. I'd never wanted to touch Drew's mouth. I'm sure it was only because the psychic had mentioned Brady's smile—correction. She'd mentioned a guy with a nice smile. I didn't know for sure if it was this guy. There were probably hundreds of guys who wore red Chiefs caps over their sandy blond hair.

He removed his cap and combed his fingers through his hair, before tucking his cap in his back pocket. Drew's hair was black, short. Brady's curled a little on the ends, fell forward over his brow. It seemed to irritate him that it did, because he combed it back a couple of more times, then shrugged. "My dad would get after me for wearing a hat indoors," he said. "So, anyway, I'll be a sophomore in the fall."

Even though he was blond, he was really tanned. I figured he liked the outdoors. Drew, even though he was dark, was pretty pale. Not vampire pale or anything, but he much preferred staying indoors.

"At Rice," I reiterated.

"Yep. We're practically neighbors, and here we meet in New Orleans. What are the odds?"

"Five million to one."

His brown eyes widened slightly. The psychic didn't mention that he had really nice eyes. A golden brown, sort of like warm, fresh pralines.

"Really?" he asked.

"No, I was just throwing out numbers. I have no idea."

He laughed. Need I say it? His laugh was nice. Everything about him was nice. And it made me uncomfortable because I didn't want to like him, not even for just one night. Because if we spent time together tonight and I never saw him again, if he didn't ask for my phone number . . . quite honestly, it would hurt. And it would add to all the insecurities that I was already harboring, because I had to have at least one flaw, maybe more. There had to be some reason that Drew abandoned me for someone else. Something had to be lacking in me.

If I'd been brave, I would have asked Drew. Why'd he do it? What was wrong with me? But part of me didn't want to know the truth, wasn't ready to face whatever it was that was wrong with me.

I actually hadn't talked to Drew at all that night after I discovered him cheating on me. I just took my cell phone off the seat, walked away, and called my dad to come pick me up.

"You okay?" Brady asked now, jerking me back to the present—which was a much nicer place to be.

"Oh, yeah. I couldn't remember if I left the iron on." It was something my mom said when she didn't want to talk about whatever it was she'd been thinking about. It made absolutely no sense and was a stupid thing to say. Still, I said it.

"You iron?" he asked incredulously.

"It's obvious you don't."

He looked down at his wrinkled shirt. "Yeah, my duffle bag was pretty stuffed, and we wanted to get in as much sightseeing as we could today."

"So you're just here for the day?"

"Nah, we're here for the summer. Volunteering, building a house, I think. Tank's got the details, I'm just along for the ride."

"That's the reason we're here, too."

There were lots of volunteer and rebuilding efforts in the city. The odds that we were going to be working on the same project could've *really* been five million to one. I was sure it wasn't happening.

So I began to relax a little. What was wrong with having fun—just for tonight?

"Do you believe in love at first sight, or should we walk by again?"

We all groaned at Tank's corny pickup line.

Sometime between the time that the server brought our food and we finished eating, we all seemed to have become friends. Or at least comfortable enough with one another for Jenna to tell Tank that she thought his line about us being their destiny was pretty corny. So the guys had started tossing out their repertoire of worst pickup lines—just to prove that Tank's hadn't been that bad.

"I hope you know CPR, 'cuz you take my breath away," Sean said. He had a really deep baritone voice that sounded like it came up from the soles of his feet.

Jenna and I laughed, but Amber looked at him like maybe she was wondering if he was serious.

He wasn't very tall. But that worked. Because neither was Amber. Not that it needed to work, because she had a boyfriend.

"Do the police have a warrant out for your arrest?" Brady asked. "Because your eyes are killing me."

I laughed.

"No, seriously," he said. "You've got really pretty brown eyes."

"Oh, that wasn't a line?"

"Well, yeah, it's a line, but I do mean it."

"Oh, well, in that case, thanks. I think."

Were we moving into flirting territory?

"You must be tired," he said, "because you've been running through my mind ever since I first saw you."

"Is that a line?" I asked, not certain if I

should laugh again.

"Not really," Tank said before Brady could answer. "We were kicking ourselves for not introducing ourselves to y'all earlier. I'm glad we ran into you again."

I watched as Jenna's cheeks turned pink. "Yeah, we're glad, too," she said.

When the server brought our bill, the guys insisted on paying for everything. Which was so nice and unexpected. I mean, they looked more like starving students than we did.

As we left the restaurant, Tank said, "We're going to hang out on Bourbon Street. Want to come?"

Jenna didn't hesitate. "Absolutely."

Even Amber seemed up for it, which left everyone looking at me. What choice did I have? I shrugged. "Sure."

No way was I going to wander around New Orleans at night alone. And it had gotten dark while we were eating. Besides, I'd heard about Bourbon Street, and I wanted to experience it.

It was obvious Jenna was really interested in Tank. They were even holding hands already.

I'd expected Amber to walk with me, but she was still paired up with Sean, talking to him as we headed over to Bourbon Street. Apparently she wasn't worried about what Chad might think, or maybe she was okay with being with a guy as a friend.

Maybe she was right. What would it hurt if tonight—just tonight—I was a little wild and crazy? If tonight, I had fun with a guy? If tonight, I pretended my heart hadn't been shattered?

Brady took my hand. His was large, warm, and comforting. But still, I jerked a little at the unexpected closeness.

"So we don't get separated," he said, as though he wanted to reassure me that nothing heavy was going on between us. "There's usually a crowd on Bourbon Street."

"I thought you were new to town."

"I am, but I know things."

Chapter 4

Several blocks of Bourbon Street were closed to traffic. The area was a mash of bodies, noises, and smells. I hadn't expected one of those noises to be the *clip clop* of horses' hooves or one of the smells to be manure.

But the police were patrolling on huge horses, and big horses left behind big business.

"Watch out," Brady said, slipping his arm around my waist and hauling me to the side before I stepped in something I absolutely didn't want to. He laughed. "I think my shoes just became disposable." Although we'd missed stepping into a big mess, the street was trashed.

"Mine, too. Definitely."

I smiled up at him, not sure why I suddenly felt very comfortable around him. Maybe it was the revelry surrounding us. Maybe it was everyone shouting and laughing and having a great time. The attitude was contagious, something I wanted to embrace.

I was suddenly very glad to be sharing all this with a guy. Not even Brady particularly, just a guy. Because it seemed like the kind of partying that required holding hands and being part of a couple.

People were acting wild, crazy, totally uninhibited. Dancing, yelling, hugging, kissing, laughing. It wasn't all because of the drinking going on. Sure, some people were drinking freely in the streets, weaving in and out of the crowds. I'm certain a lot of them were drunk on booze, but many were simply drunk on having a good time.

When everyone around you doesn't care what anyone else thinks, why should you?

A guy bumped into us, staggered back, and raised his fist in the air. "Rock on!"

He swerved away, hit a lamppost. "Rock on!"

Brady drew me nearer. "That dude's going to be seriously hung over in the morning if he already can't tell the difference between a post and a person."

"Are you speaking from experience?"

I didn't know why I asked that. It was rude. But I think I was looking for a flaw. He couldn't be this perfect. I wanted him to be not so nice.

He grinned. Obviously he didn't take offense at what I'd said.

"I refuse to answer that question on the grounds that it might incriminate me."

"What are you—a law student?"

"Architecture. We're all architecture majors. It's part of the reason we're here."

"To help rebuild."

"That, and to appreciate what remains."

He made it sound so noble, so . . . un-Drew. The only thing Drew had appreciated was the spotlight, which hadn't bothered me at the time, because it had made him—made us—seem special. I'd never considered him self-centered or selfish, but now I wasn't so sure.

Brady and I walked in tandem, following

Tank and Jenna. Their height made them easy to keep in sight.

The street didn't have a shortage of bars, which you'd probably expect of a street named Bourbon, although the name didn't really refer to booze. At the time New Orleans was founded by the French, the French royal family was the House of Bourbon and *Rue Bourbon* was named to honor them. Yes, I'd spent a lot of time on Wikipedia, looking up facts that were probably only interesting to me. Which is why I didn't share that one with Brady.

We stopped just outside a corner daiquiri bar. The huge doors were wide open. People walked in, got their drinks, and strolled out. Behind the counter were several huge vats of frozen drinks, so it didn't take very long to get served. The tables inside were crammed with people watching a baseball game on the TV hanging on the wall.

"I don't get that," Brady said.

"What?"

"You've got all this stuff happening out here, and people are in there watching TV. I can watch TV at home. Why come here if that's what you're going to do?"

"Maybe New Orleans is their home."

"Maybe."

"Or maybe they're huge baseball fans."

"Still. I believe you gotta experience life, not watch it."

He looked at me like he thought I should agree. I didn't know what to say. Up until this summer, my experiences were pretty limited. I didn't want to get into an experience-listing competition.

"I'm making a run," Tank suddenly said.

He went inside, leaving Jenna on the sidewalk. She had her cell phone out, pointed it at me, took a picture, and winked. For her MySpace page, no doubt. As proof to Drew that I'd totally gotten over him. Moved on.

Who knew pictures could lie?

It was only then that I realized I was still nestled snugly against Brady's side. I didn't want to be obvious about easing away from him, which meant that I stayed beside him because there was no way to move away without being obvious.

So, okay, maybe I was just looking for an excuse to stay close. The weight of his arm around me felt really nice.

"You're not going to get something to drink?" I asked.

He grinned and winked. "I'm not going in to *buy* something, but yeah, I'll have something. Tank's the only one who's twenty-one. I might get carded if I tried to buy it, but I don't usually get carded once I'm holding it."

I wondered if that was part of the reason he kept stubble on his chin, so he'd look older. It was considerably darker than his hair. It gave him a rough, dangerous look. Which gave me a thrill. To be with someone older, someone who looked like he could be trouble, someone who wasn't Drew.

"Sounds like you have a system," I said. There I was again, being snide, trying to find that elusive flaw. What *was* wrong with me?

"I believe in partying hearty. And tonight we're pedestrians, so the only crashing that will take place is when we hit the beds." He gave me his sexy grin. (Did he have any other kind?) "Who am I hurting?"

Tank came out with a frozen red drink.

"Strawberry daiquiri," he said. "They give a free shot of Sex on the Beach, but I couldn't bring it out, so I was forced to drink it myself."

"But you're always willing to make the sacrifice," Brady said.

"You bet! Let's party!"

We started walking up the sidewalk, stepping into the street when the crowds were thick on the sidewalk outside the bars that had entertainment. Music wafted out through the open doors. I wasn't familiar with the tunes but hearing them live made me want to follow their rhythm. I thought I could probably become a fan. Expand my musical horizons.

When we passed through some shadows, Tank passed the drink back. Brady took it and offered it to me. Okay. I wasn't old enough, but I didn't want to seem like a prude, either. I compromised and took a very small sip. It was tasty, so I took another. I was pretty sure all the alcohol was on the bottom and I'd lifted the straw up some, so I was drinking from the

middle. The alcohol-free zone. Sounded reason-
able to me. Not that a cop would buy into my
reasoning.

A vision flashed through my mind of having
to call Mom and Dad to bail me out of jail.
Wouldn't that be just great? I wondered if that
was how things worked for Saraphina. Pictures
just flashed through her mind and they could
mean nothing, something, everything. How did
she know which ones mattered?

Brady didn't bother with a straw. He just
gulped down some frozen concoction. We
passed another bar, and Tank went inside.

I looked around. "Where's Amber?"

Jenna turned in a slow circle, then shrugged.
"I don't know."

"She and Sean ducked into one of the
bars we passed back there to listen to the
music," Brady said, jerking his thumb over his
shoulder.

How had I missed that? I hadn't seen Amber
and Sean slip away. I guess maybe I was paying
too much attention to Brady. But sitting down
and listening to a band sounded like a terrific

idea. One way to keep my shoes semiclean anyway. But then, I also wanted to see everything there was to see out here, too.

"We can go back there if you want," Brady said.

He didn't say it with much enthusiasm. I didn't know him well enough to read between the lines, but I had a feeling that he wanted to keep walking. I didn't know how I knew that. I just did.

"No, I'd rather explore."

"Great! Let's at least go to the end of what they've got blocked off. See what other stuff they've got going on. Then we can head back, find the bar they're in."

"Sounds like a plan."

"I'm known for my plans."

"Really?"

"Oh yeah. That's what architects do. Draw up plans."

He gave me a smile that seemed to say I was part of those plans. Or maybe I was just reading things into his expression that I wanted to be there. Maybe he was really talking about blueprints. Although part of me was hoping for the more personal meaning. We were having a good time. And I suddenly wanted to have a good time. A really good time. Show Drew that I was finished moping about him. Have Jenna post a hundred of those pictures for him to see.

Tank came out of the bar with a yellow frozen drink. "Banana," he said, boldly offering it to Jenna.

She took it without hesitating.

We started walking up the street again.

"More?" Brady asked, holding the strawberry daiquiri toward me.

"Uh, no, but thanks."

I felt like a total downer, but my parents had let me come here because they trusted me not to get into trouble. Trust was a heavy burden, a double-edged sword. Too many clichés to name. But I didn't want to do something the first night that would have me back home the second.

Brady finished the daiquiri, crumpled up the plastic cup—why do guys always feel a need to crumple whatever they've been drinking out of?—and tossed it in a nearby trash can.

"We need to get you some beads," he said.

I was pretty sure he wasn't talking about buying me any that were hanging in the windows of the many shops.

Guys stood on balconies, dangling beads, and yelling at girls walking by. Whenever a girl lifted her top, a guy would toss her a strand or two. Unless he was totally wasted, in which case the beads landed on nearby trees or shrubbery. Beads were pretty much all over the place.

"I've decided not to do *everything* the first night," I said. "I want to leave something for later in the summer."

Brady chuckled, leaned near my ear, and whispered, "Chicken."

Okay, maybe I was. I'd never even lifted my shirt for Drew.

"Don't look so serious," Brady said. "I'm just teasing."

"I guess I don't know you well enough—"

"To share what's underneath that tee?"

"To know when you're teasing," I corrected.

"There is that."

He released his hold on me, which I realized felt strange. Not to have him holding me. I almost felt bereft. But that didn't make sense. I'd just met the guy.

He moved so he was standing near a balcony. Waving his arms, he was yelling up at the people leaning over the railing. I'd seen only guys on the balconies, but this one had girls, too. Probably in college. When Brady got their attention, he laughed and pulled his T-shirt up and over his head, then he swung it around like a lasso.

Someone bumped against me. I barely noticed.

Brady was buff. Nothing at all like Drew.

I'd tried to interest Drew in various charity runs. He'd always been willing to sponsor me if I was participating, which I'd thought was nice, but I had a feeling that Brady actually ran. And worked out, and engaged in outdoor activities. Based on the bronzed darkness of his back, I had a feeling he spent most of his time in the sun.

I watched as dozens of beads dropped

through the air. Brady snagged them. He was hamming it up, dancing around, strutting his stuff. The party girls were whistling, dropping more beads, inviting him up.

Brady was being crazy, dancing around, having fun, not caring what anyone thought.

I started laughing. He hadn't struck me as being quite so uninhibited, but it was all in the spirit of New Orleans. I think everyone around him was having as much fun as he was.

I was really, really glad that I was there, involved, part of the madness.

Brady turned toward me, holding up all the strands of beads, smiling like some returning explorer who was delivering gold to his queen or something. He dropped them down over my head.

Then, grinning broadly, he wrapped his fingers around them, pulled me toward him, and kissed me.

Right there in the middle of Bourbon Street, with people pushing past us and music filling the night.

Chapter 5

*B*rady tasted like strawberry daiquiri, and I thought his mouth should be cold from the frozen drink, but it wasn't. It was hot. Very hot.

He brought the beads and his knuckles up beneath my chin. He tilted my head back slightly and started kissing me more thoroughly.

And the thing was—I was kissing him back.

I told myself that the sip of daiquiri had gone to my head. I told myself that it was simply the craziness of Bourbon Street.

But I think part of it was that I wanted to hurt Drew. Like me kissing a guy as though my life depended on it would somehow make us even.

Which was crazy. Because Drew would

never know. And it wasn't fair to Brady. And I knew, I knew, I *knew* that I should stop kissing him. That my reasons for kissing him had nothing at all to do with him, but was some convoluted sense of revenge.

Brady was such a nice guy, with a terrific smile. And he kissed me like Drew never had. Part of me wanted to stay there forever.

But it was wrong.

I drew back.

Brady gave me a broad smile. "Oh yeah."

He leaned back in. I put my hand on his bare chest. His skin was warm and my fingers tingled. I almost moved back toward him. Instead, I said, "I've gotta go."

He looked like I'd just told him that he'd stepped in something gross. "What?"

"I have a curfew."

"A curfew?"

"Yeah, our chaperone is picking us up at the gate to Jackson Square." I looked at my watch, preparing to lie about the pickup time, but it really was almost eleven. How had that happened? Time had completely gotten away from me. "She's picking us up at eleven. I really have to go. Thanks for the beads, for dinner, for . . . everything."

The kiss, I thought, *really, really thank you for the amazing kiss.*

Turning, I hurried back the way we'd come. Or I tried to hurry. It was a little hard when I had to wedge myself between people. "Coming through. Excuse me."

"Wait, you can't just . . . go off by yourself!" I heard Brady call out.

Only I wasn't planning to go off by myself. I was planning to go with Jenna and Amber. I just had to find them.

Brady caught up with me. "Hey, come on. Slow down."

I had my phone out, trying to call Jenna. I didn't know if she'd be able to hear her cell ringing over the saxophones and horns playing their upbeat music and the din of all the people.

"Hey, Dawn, wait up." Brady grabbed my arm.

I spun around. "You're a nice guy, but—"

"It's okay. I didn't realize . . . a curfew.

Wow. Do your friends have one?"

I nodded, wishing I'd used some other excuse. I suddenly felt like such a kid. "It's not really a curfew; it's just that she's picking us up at eleven, so we need to go. Otherwise, she might give us a real curfew."

That sounded worse. Why didn't I just shut up already?

"Okay, I just wish you'd said something sooner."

If I had, he probably wouldn't have brought me to Bourbon Street at all. He probably wouldn't have kissed me.

It took us nearly twenty minutes to find everyone else. Brady didn't say anything the entire time. Didn't hold my hand, although he did keep brushing up against me when the crowds thickened. He'd put his shirt back on — thank goodness. He placed his arm around my shoulders only once and that was when some drunken guy almost stumbled into me — Brady pulled me out of the way, trying to protect me.

I kept thinking I had to be insane for not holding on to this guy with both hands. I probably could have called Ms. Wynder and . . .

what? Our first night here and we couldn't meet up for the rendezvous because we were partying too hard? I was pretty sure that wouldn't go over well.

After we found everyone, we headed for Jackson Square. Tank and Jenna were in the lead again, holding hands. Amber was with Sean, talking. Brady and I trailed behind.

"Look, about that kiss—" Brady began.

"Don't worry about it. It was no big deal."

"Ouch!"

I grimaced. That had really come off sounding bad. I wanted to be cool about it, but I didn't know how. I mean, Drew and I had dated about a month before he ever got up the courage to kiss me. I think it had been his first kiss, too, and it had been, well, awkward. Eventually, we were kissing like pros. I'm not sure pro what. Are there pro kissers?

"I just meant that I know it was the craziness of Bourbon Street that made us kiss," I said.

"You think?"

"Oh yeah. I mean, we just met. It can't be more than that."

"I guess."

"I mean, this wasn't even a date or anything. It was just hanging out."

"Okay. Yeah."

I couldn't tell if he was disappointed or relieved.

When we got near the gate, I saw the other three girls Ms. Wynder had dropped off earlier. They went to my school, too, but I didn't know them very well.

"There's our group," I told Brady.

I turned around, walking backward. "Thanks again."

A familiar minivan pulled up to the curb. Amber, Jenna, and I started running for it.

We were all eerily quiet in the minivan after Ms. Wynder asked how our day was and we all responded "Great." As though a one-word answer would suffice when it most certainly didn't.

It had been one of the most up-and-down days of my life. I'd run through the entire gamut of emotions. I was exhausted. And wondering about the psychic's prediction. Was Brady the guy? Had I seen him for the last time? Was my last memory of him going to be watching him fade into the shadows of the night?

Once we got to our dorm room, we all let out collective sighs and started preparing for bed. Even though it seemed like something needed to be said, none of us was saying anything.

I plugged in the pump and pressed the button to inflate the AeroBed that I'd be sleeping on. Each dorm room had only two beds. I had the choice of an air mattress or a roommate I didn't know—Amber and Jenna had already agreed to bunk together before I realized that I wouldn't be doing a summer tour of Texas water parks with Drew. Yeah, that had been our plan. To be together as much as possible. Slipping and sliding the summer away. It had sure sounded like fun at the time.

Since my life seemed to be a series of adjustments lately, I hadn't wanted to adjust to living with a stranger, so I'd decided to go the air mattress route.

Besides, the summer would be a lot more

fun if we were all together. Every night would be a sleepover.

Amber sat on the edge of her bed. "Okay, guys, I need y'all to promise that you'll never tell Chad what I did tonight."

Crouching on the floor by the mattress, I twisted around. "What did you do?"

"Where were *you*? I hung out with another guy!" Her voice went up a bit; it had an almost-panicked sound to it.

I know after my prom night experience, I probably should have been all over her case, but Amber was innocent. She hadn't done anything wrong, which I felt a need to point out. "Yeah, but you—what? Listened to music?"

She nodded and looked miserable.

"It's not like you were all over him, or sneaking around."

"Still, he's a guy."

"But you can have guy friends."

"Just don't say anything to Chad. Ever."

"We won't tell," Jenna said.

"Of course, we won't," I assured her. "You don't even have to ask."

"Thanks. He just so wouldn't understand."

She looked at Jenna. "What about you?"

"What about me?"

"You and Tank. Are you going to see him again?"

She shrugged. "I gave him my cell phone number, but we were in such a rush at the end, we didn't really say good-bye or make any plans—"

Her cell phone rang. She took it out of her shorts pocket and just stared at it.

"Answer it," I prodded.

"It's Tank. What do I say?"

"Hello?" I suggested.

She took a deep breath, opened her phone, and answered, "Hey."

With a big smile, she said, "Oh yeah. We're fine. I know it was crazy there at the end. I didn't realize it was so late until Dawn found us." She laughed. "No, we don't turn into pumpkins at midnight."

Rolling onto her side, she curled up and started talking really quietly.

"Should we leave the room?" Amber whispered.

"Nah. We can't head out every time one of

us gets a phone call." I turned off the pump and tested the firmness of my bed. It worked.

"What are we going to do if she keeps seeing him?" Amber asked.

"What do you mean?"

"Well, the other two guys will probably be there. I just don't know if it's such a good idea for all of us to hang out together. I mean —"

"Why don't we worry about it if it happens?"

She jerked her thumb toward Jenna. "You don't think his calling means it's going to happen?"

It probably did.

"I'm too tired to solve this right now," I told her. I just wanted to go to sleep. We'd been running around all day.

"I know I'm probably worried about nothing. Gawd, I wish we hadn't decided to visit a psychic." Amber got her stuff together and went into the bathroom.

I fingered the beads dangling around my neck. I didn't know why I'd freaked out when Brady kissed me. Yes, I did. Brady was nice and that scared me. I didn't trust him not to hurt me.

Even for one night. It was a lot easier leaving him than it would be having him leave me.

Jenna had talked about having a summer fling, but I'd never had a casual relationship. Drew had been my first date. I didn't know how to date a guy without caring about him. And why would I want to?

Why spend time with someone I didn't like? And if I liked him, well, the more time I spent with him, it seemed like the more I'd start to like him, and the next thing I'd know . . . I'd be vulnerable again.

The best thing for me to do this summer was to just hang out with Jenna and Amber. And if Jenna was with Tank all the time, then Amber and I would buddy up.

I was probably worrying for nothing.

I'd never see Brady again, anyway. Even if Jenna saw Tank, it didn't mean that Amber and I would hook up with the other guys.

Brady was no doubt going to be just a one night . . . whatever.

Chapter 6

"Okay, I've blogged day one of what I'm calling our Amazing Summer Adventure," Jenna said, leaning away from the desk where she'd set up her laptop.

It was the next morning. Ms. Wynder had knocked on our door shortly after the sun made its appearance. When I'd volunteered for this, I hadn't considered that I'd be sleep deprived the whole summer. Even when I worked for my parents, I didn't go in until just before the lunch crowd hit.

Although I suppose I wouldn't have been dragging so much if I hadn't stared into the darkness for most of the night, thinking about Brady. Reliving the kiss. Wondering if he'd decided that I was a total nut.

What did I care what he thought? I'd probably never see him again. Saraphina's predictions were no doubt all jumbled up. Visions weren't an exact science. Just because she'd mentioned hammering and a red cap didn't mean they were in proximity. Last night was probably it.

Of course, Amber, who was used to getting up with the cows—literally—was her usual perky self. She seemed to be totally over all the doubts she'd had the day before about the psychic encounter.

She and I peered over Jenna's shoulder. Jenna wanted to be a journalist, so she was all about reporting what was happening in our lives—with posting photos and all. And there was the photo of me and Brady.

I looked . . . happy. And he looked . . . sexy. And together we looked . . . cuddly. An item.

And I thought, *Drew, eat your heart out.*

"So Drew is still on your friends list?" I asked, trying not to sound as interested as I was.

"Oh, sure. He's bound to see this."

"Why?"

"Because I write interesting stuff, and he knows it. And he'll be interested. I mean, face it. What we're doing here is way different from what anyone else is doing over the summer. He'll want to know all the delicious details."

She got up from the chair and I sat down. The room didn't have much furniture except the beds, two dressers, a desk, and three chairs — two of which we'd raided from a lounge down the hall.

Amber pressed up against my back as she tried to read what Jenna had written. "You didn't mention Sean, did you?"

"Of course not."

Jenna had written about our visit with the psychic but glossed over her prediction for Amber — no doubt because Chad was on her friends list, too, and he didn't need to know that Amber might find someone better.

Jenna hadn't revealed anything incriminating. Still, it always unsettled me a little to see the intimate details of my life shared with others.

"Oh, by the way," Jenna said as she started getting dressed, "I might see Tank tonight."

I could hear the excitement in her voice.

"Where?" I asked, trying to sound casually interested, instead of anxious to know if that meant that I might see Brady. Did I want to see him? I did. Scary.

Amber moved away to start getting dressed, too. I decided I'd better follow or I'd be left behind. I pulled on the Helping Hands Helping Humans T-shirt that Ms. Wynder had designed for us to wear the first day to identify our group. It had hands all over it. What can I say? She was more into numbers than art.

Jenna shrugged. "I'm supposed to figure out exactly where the dorm is and call him later with directions. He has a car. Said he'd come get me."

"That's awesome!" Amber said at the same time I said, "Aren't things moving a little fast?"

I never would have asked that question before prom night. Sometimes I missed the old me.

"I mean—"

"I know," Jenna said. "You got hurt and now you don't trust boys, and you're worried that I'll get hurt, too."

"I trust boys." I trusted them to hurt me. Drew had really messed me up. I hated that I was giving him that power.

I sat on a chair and started lacing up my

hiking boots. We'd been warned to wear sturdy shoes and jeans because we didn't know what we'd run across in the debris. No exposed legs. No sandals.

"You don't trust boys," Jenna repeated.

What was I supposed to say to that? Do, too? So we could get into exchanging meaningless comebacks like two-year-olds?

"Uh, y'all, do we *have* to wear these T-shirts?" Amber asked.

I looked over at her and saw that the hands on her T-shirt were rudely placed. I dropped my gaze to my own chest. Yep, those little hands were sending a message that I didn't want to send.

Jenna started laughing. "Oh my gosh. I never thought I'd be so glad for a tall body. At least my hands aren't exactly where they shouldn't be."

"Considering the message, I don't think we do need to wear them," I said. "At least I'm not."

I jerked off my T-shirt and scrounged around in my suitcase until I found a faded T-shirt from a vacation my family had taken at Thrill Ride! Amusement Park.

Amber and Jenna changed their shirts, too.

I welcomed the distraction from what might have turned into an argument with Jenna. I was really happy for her, glad she'd met a guy who wasn't bothered by her height. And I really, really hoped . . .

I didn't know what I hoped. That she didn't get hurt, of course, because we were only here for the summer, and he was only here for the summer, and even though he went to college in Houston. . . . I suppose their relationship could last past our time in New Orleans. As a matter of fact, before prom night, I probably would have *believed* in it continuing after we got home. But I used to believe in a lot of good things, like love was forever and boyfriends were neat to have.

Pancakes and sausages were waiting for us in the cafeteria. Several of the volunteers were already eating. Our little group of six, along with Ms. Wynder, gathered at one table. While we ate, Ms. Wynder went over the safety rules again: Watch out for critters, stay alert, don't get in a hurry, haste makes waste, the usual stuff. When we were finished eating, we headed outside, climbed into her minivan, and caravanned with the other volunteers to the site.

We were silent as we drove along, looking out the windows at the devastation. Walking through the French Quarter yesterday, having fun, it was easy to forget how ruined other parts of New Orleans still were. But we could also see the areas that had already been rebuilt. They spoke to the strength and determination of the people of the city.

As my admiration for them was growing, my cell phone rang. I pulled it out of the case attached to my belt. My dad had given me the case because he thought it would make it easier to keep my phone handy and he didn't want me to be without quick access to it. "In case of an emergency."

So maybe he and Mom *were* a little worried about me being away from home—at least, that's what occurred to me when I saw Mom's name pop up in the window.

"Hey," I said, after answering.

"What's going on?" Mom asked curtly.

Her question wasn't at all friendly. Not a *what's happening?* It was more of a *what trouble are you getting into?*

I was sitting on the backseat between Amber and Jenna. They must have heard her through the phone because they both looked at me.

"What do you mean?" I asked.

"Drew e-mailed me a picture of you with some guy —"

"He did what?" That jerk! Why would he do that?

"He sent me —"

"Sorry, Mom," I interrupted again. Mom hated being interrupted, but she was almost four hundred miles away. What could she do, other than growl? "I got you the first time. My question was more of a 'what was he thinking.'"

"So who is this guy?"

"Just someone I met."

She was quiet for a minute. It was never good when Mom was quiet.

"He's a student at Rice," I felt compelled to explain. "He's here for the summer doing the same thing we are."

"Does Ms. Wynder know him?"

Define know, I thought. She'd seen him if she'd been looking out her window last night at the precise moment needed to see him before he disappeared.

"Yes."

I squeezed my eyes shut, hoping she wouldn't ask to speak with Ms. Wynder.

"It's just that I know you're still not over Drew—"

"I am over Drew," I interrupted.

"—and I don't want you doing anything stupid," Mom finished.

"I won't. Don't worry."

Of course, do we ever *plan* to do something stupid? It's not like I wake up in the morning and think, "Today would be a good day to do something stupid."

"It's a mother's job to worry," Mom said. "I just need reassurance there isn't any craziness going on."

"None whatsoever. Please don't worry, Mom. I'm fine. We're in the van now, heading to the site." I thought trying to distract her would be a good move on my part. "We're looking forward to helping to clean things up."

"Yet you don't seem to care about cleaning your room. What's wrong with this picture?"

I could tell that she was teasing and had gotten past whatever had been bothering her. We talked for a little while longer, then said good-bye. I told Jenna and Amber what Drew had done.

"Why would he do that?" Jenna asked.

I shrugged, surprised that he cared what I was doing. I hadn't *really* thought that he'd read Jenna's blog. Why would he? We were so over. Why would he care?

"He's definitely coming off my friends list," Jenna said.

I didn't say anything, but I thought he should have come off sooner.

"Everything all right back there?" Ms. Wynder asked.

"Yes, ma'am. Just my mom missing me."

And my ex-boyfriend trying to stir up trouble.

Chapter 7

*O*ur caravan pulled to a stop in a neighborhood that still reflected the aftermath of the storm. The street had been cleared of debris, but what remained of the houses littered the yards.

No one said anything as we climbed out of the van. I thought I was prepared for this, but I wasn't. It seemed like an impossible task, and yet I was also filled with a sense that we could make a difference. We could get this done.

"Hey!" a guy called out in a welcoming way. "Everyone over here!"

He was standing on a ladder, near the first house on the block, urging us over. He was older, much older. Probably as old as Ms.

Wynder. He wore a black T-shirt with the French fleur-de-lis on the front above the words "Rebuild New Orleans." He had curly red hair that fluffed out beneath his white cap and made him look a little like a clown. All he needed was the red nose—only his was very white, covered in zinc oxide.

Another caravan of vehicles pulled up. I found myself standing on tiptoe, trying to see if I recognized anyone from the dorm or breakfast that morning. Okay, that wasn't exactly true. I was searching for someone I'd seen yesterday, last night to be precise. I was pathetic. I didn't really know what I wanted. To see him again, to never see him again.

I knew he probably wouldn't be at the site, but there was one irritating little spark of hope that wouldn't have been disappointed if he showed up.

And then I saw someone I recognized, the very last person I'd expected to see here.

"Hey, is that—" Amber began.

"The psychic," Jenna finished.

"Hey, Sara! Bring your group over here,"

the guy on the ladder yelled.

Waving at him, she herded her little group over. Wearing jeans and a tank top, with her red hair pulled back in a ponytail, she looked like a normal person. Her group was mostly guys, which was pretty understandable because she was really pretty—gorgeous actually. It took me a minute to realize that, because I was scanning the guys following her.

Okay, I was doing more than scanning. I was seriously searching for the familiar red cap, the nice smile. Which was dumb, because if I wanted to see Brady again, all I had to do was tell Jenna and she'd call Tank and he'd tell Brady and Brady could call me . . . only I didn't know if that's what I wanted.

But I didn't see anyone I recognized.

"Why is she here?" Amber asked. "Is she going to do psychic readings?"

"Based on the way she's dressed, she's probably here for the same reason we are," I said.

"That's weird," Jenna said.

"Not really," I said. "I mean, people who live in New Orleans are working to rebuild it, too."

"Still, a psychic," Jenna said. "Do you think she'll let us know if she gets bad vibes?"

Before I could respond, the guy on the ladder clapped his hands. "All right, people! I need your attention!"

Everyone stopped talking and edged up closer.

The guy clapped his hands again. "I'm John. And this house is our project." He pointed toward the house behind him. "Working together, we're going to gut it, then rebuild it."

Gut it. That sounded so harsh.

"Gutting should take only a couple of days. We're going to move everything out, put it at the edge of the street so we can haul it away. We're going to remove the walls, the windows, the doors. The only thing we'll leave is what remains of the frame."

We'll be able to do all that in a couple of days? I thought. Amazing.

"The woman who lives here is staying with her parents right now. She's already taken all that's salvageable, so anything else—just move it to the curb. Be sure to gear up. We have hard hats, safety goggles, and dust masks over there. Work together and be really careful because you don't know what you're going to find hidden beneath all this stuff."

Hidden? A shiver went through me. Saraphina had said I'd find something hidden.

"Any questions, people?" Without hesitating a beat, he clapped his hands three times. "Then let's go!"

"I had a question," Amber said.

"Did you really?" I asked.

She smiled. "No, but he didn't even give us a chance to ask one if we did."

"Guess he's anxious for us to get started." I caught a glimpse of Jenna off to the side, talking on her phone. I took out the work gloves that I'd stuffed into my jeans pocket earlier. Ms. Wynder had given us tips for how we needed to prepare for this summer of labor. She'd done it last year as well, so she knew what was useful and what to expect. I tugged on the gloves, grateful that I had them. Jenna came back over. She and Amber tugged on their gloves.

Then we walked over to get the rest of

our equipment. A line had already formed. Probably two dozen people were here, many already starting to walk by with their gear in place.

"Does a hard hat leave a hard-hat line around your head when you take it off?" I asked.

"What does it matter?" Jenna asked. "You're not trying to impress anyone."

"Still, with all the gear, we're going to look like we're going into a contaminated zone."

"We probably are—with the mold and stuff," Amber said.

Once we were properly geared up, we grabbed one of the wheelbarrows at the edge of the property and rolled it closer to the house.

"Why don't you girls pick up some of the loose debris that's still around the house?" John asked.

I saluted him. He grinned.

"You okay with us just tossing stuff off the porch and letting you take care of it?" he asked.

"Works for me," I said.

"Good. I love a can-do attitude."

He walked into the house and several people tromped in after him. Amber, Jenna, and I began gathering any broken and rotting pieces of wood that hadn't yet been hauled to the curb. Beneath one board, we found a doll's head, which made us sad thinking of a little girl without her doll.

John came outside and tossed what looked like molding cushions onto the ground.

"Did a little girl live here?" I asked.

He glanced over at me. "Yeah, she's fine. There are two girls, actually. They're with their mom."

"How old are they?" I asked.

"Four and six, I think."

"I guess they have new dolls now."

"Yeah, but little girls can never have too many, right?"

I smiled at him, wondering how he knew what I was thinking. "Right. If I bought something for them, would you be able to get it to them?"

"You could give it to them yourself. When we're finished, we'll welcome them home.

You'll get to meet them then."

"Oh, cool."

I hadn't realized we'd be doing that. I went back to work, picking things up. I was carefully placing the remains of a clay jar in the wheelbarrow when I heard, "Smile!"

I looked up. Jenna snapped a picture and then laughed.

"You look like someone doing something she shouldn't," she said. "Let's try this again."

"Why do you need a picture? I'm all scruffy looking."

"For one—my MySpace page. But I also want to send a pic to your mom so she can see you're hard at work and it'll calm her worries. So smile."

"I'm wearing a mask. You can't even see my mouth."

"So smile, anyway."

Smiling while picking up trash was kind of like those people who smiled in commercials selling exercise machines. It wasn't natural. Still, I pulled down my mask, gave a big fake smile, and a huge thumbs-up.

"That'll do it," Jenna said. "I'm going to see what else I can document."

She walked away. I pulled up my mask and returned to my task. I was reaching down, wrapping my hands around what looked to be a massive table leg attached to a small section of dining table, when I heard a deep voice I recognized say, "Need help with that?"

I jerked up, stepped back. My foot landed on an old board that wobbled. I teetered and would have fallen, except strong hands wrapped around my arms, steadying me.

"Careful," Brady said in a voice that fell between concerned and amused.

"What are you doing here?" I asked.

He was wearing sunglasses so I couldn't read his eyes. Some sort of white powder was sprinkled over his burgundy T-shirt. *Maybe that's his flaw*, I thought. *Maybe he does drugs.*

And how had he even realized it was me, with all my gear on? Had he noticed me when I'd posed for the camera?

"I told you yesterday. I came to volunteer," he said.

"But this site?"

He shrugged. "It's where they sent me."

"So you're into snow?" Wasn't that what they called it? Or was it blow?

"Love snow. Went skiing over spring break."

"I was referring to the powder." I pointed to his chest, trying not to remember how nice it had looked last night without a shirt covering it.

Glancing down, he started dusting off his shirt. "Oh, that. Powdered sugar. We went to Café Du Monde for beignets. Place was packed. It's the reason we're late." He looked up. "You thought it was drugs?"

I felt so silly. Talking to him through the mask. Looking at him through the goggles. Accusing him of dumb stuff.

"I was teasing."

And if you believe that, I have some swampland I could sell you.

He grinned, like he knew I was out of control, but he was willing to tolerate it.

"You eaten there yet?" he asked, taking the conversation back to his breakfast.

"No."

"It's a must-do."

"They feed us breakfast in the dorm."

"Doesn't mean you have to eat there."

Why was I discouraging a hot guy from showing interest in me?

And why was he interested in me?

Why not?

I felt like the before-Drew me and the after-Drew me were on the debate team. And doing a pretty lousy job at substantiating arguments.

"Are you staying at the dorm?" I asked. It would be totally weird if he was, that everything—fate, the dating gods, whatever—was putting him in my path.

"Nah, we've got some cheap rooms in a small hotel in the French Quarter. Tank knew some people who knew some people." He shrugged.

"Is he in charge of your group?"

"We're not official, not really organized. As a matter of fact, very unorganized. Tank asked if I wanted to come to New Orleans for the summer and do some volunteer work, said he'd secured some beds, and since I had nothing better to do—here I am." He made a grand sweeping gesture. "At your service. So let me help you with this."

"But you're not geared up."

"I'll gear up in a minute. Let's get this done."

Squatting, he grabbed the end of the table leg that was still attached to part of the table.

I bent over—

"It's better for your back if you use your legs to lift stuff," he said.

"My toes don't hold things well."

He laughed. "Funny. You grab with your hands, but lift with your legs. See?"

He demonstrated, his legs doing a smooth pumping action, like a piston. He had really nice thighs. Even covered in jeans, they looked firm. Very firm.

"So, you're what? A lifting coach?" I asked.

"Nah. I worked for an overnight package deliverer over winter break. Had to watch safety videos." He shifted the table leg so he was able to carry it by himself and drop it in the wheelbarrow.

It was only then that I noticed Tank and

Jenna working together to remove a screen from a window. How it had managed to remain attached, I couldn't imagine. Most were gone, or hanging lopsided.

"Where's Amber?" I called out to Jenna.

"She went to talk to Sara/Saraphina. I think she wants another psychic reading."

"Now?" I asked.

Jenna shrugged as she walked over to me. "She's still bummed about what Saraphina told her yesterday."

"You had a psychic reading?" Brady asked.

Now it was my turn to shrug. "It's like eating at Café Du Monde. Something you have to do when you're in New Orleans."

"What did she tell you?"

"Nothing that made any sense. Do you believe in that sort of thing?"

"Not really." He reached down, picked up a brick, and dropped it in the wheelbarrow.

Apparently, I had a new partner for the day—whether I wanted him or not.

Chapter 8

"Okay, so her real name is Sara, and Saraphina is, like, her stage name or something. She said it all has to do with marketing," Amber said.

It was a little past noon, and we were all sitting on the curb, eating deli sandwiches called po'boys that one of the local eateries had sent over. Apparently some of the restaurants provided food for the volunteers, which made it really nice on our budgets. It also gave us such a sense of being appreciated—not that we were doing any of this for kudos, but still, it was nice.

"So, did she give you another reading?" I asked.

"No. She doesn't give freebies, and she

doesn't do readings when she's outside the shop. She's just a normal person today—or as normal as she can be with two different colored eyes, but whatever. She said I'm trying too hard to interpret what she saw. I don't know how I can *not* interpret"—she darted a quick glance at Sean, who was attacking his ham sandwich— "what she told me."

I wondered if she thought that since Sean was in college, he had the potential to be the better love.

"It's not like psychic-ism—or whatever you call it—is an exact science," I reassured Amber. "She puts a thought in your mind and then when something similar—"

"Similar? Red Kansas City Chiefs hat is pretty specific," she interrupted.

"What?" Brady asked, taking off his cap and looking at the logo on the front, like he was trying to confirm that it was there.

Before lunch, we'd all taken off our gear and washed up with a water hose. He'd put his cap back on then. I'd put mine on too, because of course I had hard-hat hair.

"Saraphina said Dawn would meet a guy—" Amber began.

"She said she saw a red cap—" I interrupted.

"Close enough."

"What happens with you and the red cap?" Brady asked, settling it back into place.

"Nothing. And look"—I turned my attention back to Amber—"nothing that she saw for Jenna has shown up."

"Maybe it has and we just haven't recognized it."

"You know, I heard a story once about a guy who went to see a fortune-teller," Tank said. "He wanted to know how he was going to die. She told him that cancer would kill him. So he's looking in the mirror one day and sees this strange-colored lump on the end of his nose. He's sure it's cancer and he panics. Jumps in the car, heads to his doctor, and on the way, he's hit by an eighteen-wheeler. Game over."

"So the fortune-teller was wrong," Jenna said.

Tank shrugged. "Maybe, but in a way, cancer *did* kill him."

"That's kinda convoluted," Amber said.

"Exactly," Tank said, "but that's the way all this mumbo jumbo works. You can read anything into it that you want, and practically force what was predicted to happen."

"So you're saying that I'm overreacting," Amber said.

"I'm saying you're letting her mess with your head."

"You don't believe in psychics?"

He grinned. "I didn't say that."

"I just really wish we hadn't gone there at all."

I knew Amber was a worrier, but she'd never believed in stuff like this before. Why was she so troubled now? It made no sense.

I took a long sip of water. I was drinking water like there was no tomorrow.

"I can't believe that y'all were assigned to the same site we were," I said. "What are the odds?"

"Five million to one," Brady said, grinning.

I'd known him less than twenty-four hours and already we had a private joke. I couldn't remember what private joke Drew and I had—or if we'd even had one.

"Are you kidding? The odds were stacked in our favor. Jenna called and told me where y'all were working," Tank said.

I didn't know whether to stare at Jenna or glare at Brady. Jenna was leaning against Tank's shoulder like he was the only thing supporting her, and Brady was studying his sandwich like he was trying to determine what lunch meats they'd stuffed between the French bread.

"You called them?" I said.

"Oh yeah," Jenna said. "They're not with a group like we are. They're like freelancers or something. Just helping where needed, so I called him this morning right after we got here to see if they wanted to help out."

"John was a little freaked that we were here and not on his list. That guy is way too tightly wired," Tank said. "Apparently there are people you're supposed to contact to be an official volunteer, but"—he shrugged—"John decided having our muscles was more important than following the rules."

"It'd be insane to turn away someone wanting to help," Jenna said.

"Exactly the point we made. Who'd have thought we'd even have to argue?"

"John's Sara's brother," Amber announced.

"Really?" I asked.

"According to Sara."

"Guess she wouldn't say it if it wasn't true. Now that you've told me, I can see the resemblance, sort of," I said.

"I asked him if he could see things, but he said no," Amber said. "He said that's Sara's burden."

"I imagine it would be hard to see things, to know things," Jenna said. "It's hard enough just knowing the little bit she told us."

"All right, people!" John yelled. "Five more minutes and we need to get back to work!"

"So much for the Big *Easy*," Sean said.

We all smiled.

"You got that right," Tank said.

Amber smiled at Sean, then dropped her gaze to watch a centipede walking between her feet. Her cheeks turned red, like she was embarrassed to have Sean's attention. Or maybe it was just the heat, which was turning us all red.

The day was only half over and I wanted a shower already. With lots and lots of soap. A bubble shower. I smiled at the thought of filling a shower all the way up with water and swimming in it.

"A dip in a pool would be nice right about now," Brady said.

And I had a vision of him in the water-filled shower with me, and we were cavorting around like seals or something. Way too much imagination.

"Ookay!" I said, standing. "Think I'm ready to get back to work."

I started the exodus from the curb. Everyone crumpled up the sandwich wrappers and tossed them into a nearby trash bin. Then we went back to picking up the debris brought out of the house and putting it into a wheelbarrow. When it was full, the guys hauled it over to the curb and dumped the stuff there.

"I think we've got the absolute best team out here," Jenna said.

She was using the time when the guys went to empty the wheelbarrow to catch her breath. Okay, we all did. But her gaze followed them a little more closely.

"So you really like Tank," I said, although my voice went a little high at the end, and it came off sounding like a question.

"Yeah, I do. And I think Brady might be the one Saraphina was talking about for you. It's obvious that he likes you."

"Or I could just be convenient. You like Tank. He hangs out with Tank. I hang out with you. It's just serendipity."

"Come on. He's here, helping us, just like Saraphina predicted."

"Actually, you sort of orchestrated that, by inviting them. And Sara didn't say anything really happened with me and the guy. She just said she saw him."

"*Whatever*. We could all have so much fun together!"

I know she thought I was being difficult,

stubborn. And maybe I was. But I'd learned the hard way that you can't tell by looking if a guy is destined to hurt you. From the outside, they all look nice.

By about two o'clock, I was hot, sweaty, and ready for another break.

"All right, people," John called out, from atop his ladder. "Can I have your attention?" He made sweeping arm gestures, trying to get us all to come closer.

Jenna, Amber, and I sort of migrated together.

"Wonder what's going on?" Jenna asked.

I shook my head. I didn't have a clue.

"We're making great progress, people," John said. "But we worry that if we work you too hard, you won't come back."

Everyone laughed.

"Soooo . . . you have the rest of the afternoon off."

Applause, a few roars of approval, and some whistles followed that announcement.

John waved us into silence. "For anyone

who's interested, Sara arranged a swamp tour! The bus will be in front of Sara's shop in about"—he made a big production of looking at his watch—"forty-five minutes. Whether you go to the swamp or just hang loose, enjoy your afternoon. Tomorrow morning come back ready to hit it hard again!"

People began to disperse.

"Hmm. Swamp," Jenna murmured. "What do you think? Do we want to go to a swamp?"

"I watched an old movie called *Swamp Thing* with my dad once. That's all I know about them," I said.

"A swamp seems like such an icky thing," Amber said.

"Okay, so what do we want to do?" Jenna asked.

I shrugged. "Maybe we could go down to the French Quarter—"

"Hey, Jenna," Tank called out, walking toward us. "We're going on the tour. Are you?"

"Yeah, we are," Jenna said.

Okay, I guess our plans changed.

"Great! See you at the bus."

She waved at him as he walked away. I watched as he joined up with Brady and Sean, said something to them. Then they headed to his car.

"Hope you don't mind," Jenna said.

"I'm good with it," Amber said. "I mean, we're here to work *and* have fun."

They both looked at me, like they thought I was going to argue with the fun part. I guessed there was no reason why I *had* to go. But I didn't want to spend the rest of the afternoon alone either.

"It'll be interesting," I said enthusiastically. I didn't see how, but I was trying to be a good sport. "But I have an important question here — what *does* one wear to a swamp?"

Ms. Wynder took us back to the dorm so we could clean up — fast. She wasn't going on the tour, but she was willing to drop us off at Sara's.

'I changed into shorts. I decided to double layer two tank tops that I had, putting a red one over a pink one that peeked out just a bit. I slipped on my red sandals.

"You know a swamp is probably squishy," Jenna said.

"Yeah, you're right." I changed into sneakers. I didn't want muck getting between my toes.

Quite a crowd was at Sara's when Ms. Wynder dropped us off. The other three girls in our group immediately headed toward three guys who'd shown up at the site with Sara that morning.

"Wow, that didn't take them long," Amber said.

"Looks like a lot of people are pairing off," Jenna said.

"Here we go, everyone!" Sara said as the bus pulled up.

"I guess we can all sit together," Jenna said.

She said it like it was a fate worse than death, obviously worried that Tank wasn't there yet. And then suddenly there he was, grinning broadly, Brady and Sean right behind him.

"Hey," Tank said, taking Jenna's hand. "This is going to be awesome."

Maybe swamps were a guy thing.

Brady and Sean were both standing there with their hands in their back pockets, like they weren't exactly sure what to do. Like maybe they were wondering if we were all going to pair up again like we had last night.

I remembered how worried Amber had been about how things would play out if Jenna was seeing Tank. I hadn't wanted to deal with it then. I still didn't.

We headed onto the luxury bus. Each row had two seats. Sean was leading the way. Amber was following him. I was behind her. Sean dropped down onto a row, reached out, took Amber's hand, and pulled her down beside him. I felt a small spark of panic. Where was I supposed to go now?

I went a couple of rows back and took a seat by the window. Jenna slid onto the seat in front of me, and Tank sat beside her. That was cool. I could sit alone.

But suddenly Brady was there. He eased down beside me.

"I think the bus is going to be packed," Brady said. "Tight fit for everyone, so I figured sitting by someone I knew beat sitting by a stranger."

"These are all people from the site. Don't you know them?"

"Some of 'em, sure, but not like I know you."

What exactly did that mean?

"So should I move?" he asked.

I shook my head. "No, you're fine."

He grinned, wiggled his eyebrows. "Some would say I'm better than fine."

I couldn't help myself. I laughed.

Sara took a head count, and then the bus headed out.

"So . . . Sara predicted I'd walk into your life?" he asked in a low voice.

"Uh, no, she predicted a red baseball hat was in my future. Not exactly the same thing."

"That's weird, though."

"Yeah."

"I mean, how many Chiefs caps could be in the city?" Before I could answer, his grin broadened. "Let me guess. Five million?"

I smiled, shrugged. I didn't want to be

unfriendly. But I didn't want to be too friendly.

"What else did she say?" he asked.

"Not much. That things were a mess. There'd be hammering. Pretty vague."

"And pretty general. That could pretty much apply to anyone."

"That's what I thought. It was interesting, but not something I want to do on a regular basis."

"Well, I'm all about interesting and having fun."

I scowled at him. "But a swamp? Really. How much fun can we have at a swamp?"

"As much as we want."

Chapter 9

*H*oney Island Swamp. I liked the name—the Honey Island part at least sounded sweet—but I still couldn't get past my image of a swamp being, well, a swamp.

It was located almost an hour from New Orleans. I wasn't sure what I'd been expecting. Maybe taking a look at slime covered water from a dock and moving on. Swatting at a few mosquitoes, shooing away flies. Heading back to the Big Easy.

But no, we were getting out *on* the swamp, in a boat. And I soon discovered that the sounds out there were a different kind of music than what we'd heard in the city. Here it was the croak of bullfrogs—some were disgustingly huge and ugly—and the chirp of crickets. There were mysterious knocks and pecks and little trills. Luckily Sara had brought lots of insect repellent for anyone who wanted it. I'd slathered, sprayed, and squirted it on. I was taking no chances. I was not into bugs.

And we were at a very bug-infested place.

We climbed aboard a large, covered boat, like the kind I'd ridden once at a safari ride at a theme park—except this one was real. It didn't run along a rail. It had a motor and a captain, who steered it through the swamp.

Benches lined all four sides of the boat. We all worked our way around the deck. I managed to get a seat near the front of the boat. Brady sat beside me.

I was turned sort of sideways on the bench, so I could see clearly things that approached our side. Brady was twisted around, too, which almost had us spooning.

"You smell really nice," he said in a low voice.

"It's the insect repellent."

"It is?" Out of the corner of my eye, I could

see him sniffing the back of his hand. "Oh God, it is. How sick is that—to like the smell of insect repellent?"

I laughed. "Pretty sick."

"But admit it. You were thinking I smelled good, too."

Okay, I had been, but I wasn't going to admit it. "Maybe."

The motor cranked to life and the boat glided away from the dock. I was surprised that the water looked more like what you'd find in a river than what you might expect to find in a swamp.

Our guide was native to the area, and he shared a lot of the history—especially about pirates and Big Foot sightings—as we journeyed deeper into the swamp. Because so much of the area was protected, he explained, Honey Island Swamp was one of the least-altered river swamps in the country. It probably looked the same more than two hundred years ago when pirates were hiding out there.

"Wow," I whispered. There was an awesome beauty to the place. Huge cypress trees rose from the water.

And I'd expected the marshes to smell . . . well, like stagnant water. There was a little of that, but there was also the scent of wild azaleas. I hadn't expected the sweet fragrance.

"Look," Brady said, pointing.

At first I thought it was a log, resting at the edge of the bank, barely visible through the tall grasses. But it was an alligator. A very large alligator.

"We have more than a million alligators in Louisiana," the guide said.

"Imagine if they ever decided to band together," Brady said. "They could take over the state."

"I think I've seen that in a movie."

"Me, too. I can never get enough of giant alligator movies."

"Really?"

"Oh yeah, the bigger the creature the better. *Night of the Lepus*. A classic."

My dad was a huge creature-feature watcher, so I'd pretty much seen them all.

"Now, see, I didn't get that one. What's

scary about a bunny rabbit?" I asked.

"It's a big, big bunny rabbit."

"Still, not scary."

The guide warned us to keep all our limbs inside the boat. Then he began making a sound I'd never heard before. Alligators—the ones I'd spotted and ones that had been hidden—began slipping into the water and gliding toward the boat.

"Ohmigod!" I couldn't help it. There were so many. I imagined them tipping the boat over. I'd definitely watched too many bad movies with my dad if I really thought that was going to happen.

"It's okay," Brady said, putting his arm around me, squeezing my shoulder.

He was so comforting. But this wasn't a date. It was a group outing, and we were all sitting close together. It was just natural to reassure each other that we weren't about to become alligator dinner.

The guide began tossing something toward the alligators and the *clack* of their mouths snapping shut filled the air.

"Is he tossing marshmallows?" I asked.

"Looks like."

"How did anyone find out that they like marshmallows?"

"Beats me."

Every now and then we'd come in close to the shore, and we'd see other animals: deer, red wolves, raccoons, beavers, turtles . . . and always the alligators.

"I don't think I'd want them for neighbors," I said quietly.

"Me either."

We saw an egret and other birds. It was an untouched paradise. I knew New Orleans had once been swampland, and I wondered if it had looked like this at one time. Hard to imagine.

I looked over my shoulder to see Sara sitting near the captain. I figured we were safe. She wouldn't get on the boat if she saw danger, would she? On the other hand, her visions were so cryptic. Maybe she just saw herself swimming and didn't realize it meant she'd be swimming with the gators.

Amber and Sean were sitting together. He

was pointing stuff out to her. She was smiling. They were just being friendly. Having fun. Like me and Brady. No big deal.

Jenna and Tank were sitting close, his arms around her as they looked out at the swamp. There was no doubt that Tank was really interested in her.

I turned my attention back to the alligators. Sometimes nature was so powerful, you had no defense against it.

It was early evening when we got back to Sara's, and Ms. Wynder was there, waiting for us. Before anyone could say anything, she said, "I've made reservations for eight o'clock. We need to get moving."

Jenna didn't bother to hide her disappointment as she waved good-bye to Tank. I thought Amber looked relieved. I knew I was. It gave me time to think, to try to figure out what, if anything, was happening with Brady and me. We all got along, so I could see our little group hanging out together. But at the same time, did I need to explain to him that more kisses weren't in our future?

On the other hand, did I really want to give that up?

After we were seated at the restaurant and had given our orders to the waitress, Ms. Wynder folded her arms on the table. She looked incredibly serious.

"All right, girls, we need to talk," she said.

I wondered what we'd done wrong. Everyone looked guilty.

"I know some of you are developing . . . friendships." She paused and looked at each of us.

I wanted to raise my hand and say, "Not me!"

But the truth was that maybe I was. A little.

"During the week, curfew is midnight. On Saturday, two o'clock. I already have all your cell phone numbers"—she held up her phone as though to demonstrate—"and I want phones to be kept on at all times."

"What about when we're at a movie?" one of the other girls said.

"Vibrate. I will be making room checks. Or stop by my room and let me know when you get in. Are there any questions?"

It sounded pretty straightforward to me.

She smiled. "All right then. Tell me about the swamp."

The next day, it seemed like the sun had moved a million miles closer to earth. How else could it be so much hotter?

Or maybe it was just that we were working harder. We were actually beginning to see progress. John had given crowbars to some of the guys to start ripping off the outer walls.

Jenna had muttered, "Sexist!"

So Tank had given her his crowbar. Or let her work the crowbar with him. He'd put his arms around her and together they'd ratchet off boards. Boards that Amber and I would pick up after they were tossed to the side, put them in the wheelbarrow, and haul them to the curb.

I caught Brady watching me a time or two. Today he was geared up so much that the only thing that gave him away was when his head was turned in my direction. It felt as if he was studying me, trying to figure me out.

What was there to figure out?

We'd had fun at the swamp yesterday, but it hadn't been anything serious. And it hadn't ended in a kiss like the first night. Actually it hadn't had any type of real ending.

There had just been stepping off the bus and Ms. Wynder ushering us away like a hen going after her chicks. And all of us too surprised to say anything other than "See you tomorrow."

And even though we'd seen each other earlier today, our greeting had been a little cautious. Just a *hey*. Like we were both trying to figure out if yesterday had been more than just hanging out together because of convenience.

Do you like me?

Should I like you?

Where do we go from here?

Should we go from here?

I really wasn't sure. Last night, when I'd asked Amber why she'd hooked up with Sean, she'd said, "Everyone was pairing up. It would have been rude not to."

But if you kept pairing up with the same

person, didn't you eventually become a *couple*? I didn't want to be part of a couple. I didn't want expectations.

Hooking up one night when I didn't expect to see him again was one thing. Hooking up twice was creeping toward dangerous territory.

I thought maybe Amber was feeling the same way, too, because she was staying pretty near me today, helping me haul the debris to the curb.

It kept getting hotter and hotter, and by late afternoon, it was miserable.

John announced that we could quit for the day, but we were so close to being finished with the gutting that everyone protested. We all wanted to stay and get the job done.

Brady, Tank, and Sean walked to their car—a black Honda Civic—pulled their tees off, and tossed them inside. Not that I blamed them. All our shirts were damp from the humidity and our efforts. I thought about how nice it would feel to have the breeze blowing over exposed, damp skin.

They tossed their gear onto a table. I guess

they'd had enough of being safe. They wanted to be not so hot.

Carrying their crowbars, they headed back toward the house. I really tried not to stare at Brady's chest. It had looked nice in the shadows of Bourbon Street, but now there were no shadows. And he was definitely in shape.

Tank walked past us, touching Jenna's shoulder as he went by. "Jenna, help me out over here, will you?"

Only Jenna didn't move. Neither did Amber. Neither did I, for that matter. We were staring at Tank's back. His right shoulder, to be precise.

A shoulder that sported a tattoo of a blue and green flying dragon.

A dragon breathing fiery red and blue flames.

Fire that didn't burn.

Chapter 10

"*I* know you must think I'm insane, but I just can't help it."

Following an afternoon that seemed to have way too many hours—and surprises—in it, we were back at the dorm. Jenna and I were standing in our room, speechless, watching as Amber tossed all her stuff into her suitcase.

"I mean, red Chiefs cap"—she pointed at me—"fire that doesn't burn?" She pointed at Jenna. "I don't care what you say, there is something to that psychic reading. I've got to go home and figure out if things between Chad and me are real or over."

She'd freaked out when she'd seen Tank's tattoo. She'd told Ms. Wynder that her mother called and her grandma had died.

That afternoon, her mother *had* called, to see how things were going, after Amber had left a panicked message on her voice mail saying that she was homesick and wanted to fly home—immediately, that night, the first flight out that she could get.

And her grandmother *had* died—five years ago.

"She didn't say you were going to break up with Chad," I pointed out.

"She said I was going to find something better."

"Well, if there is something better, isn't now the time to find out?" Jenna asked. "You're only in high school—"

"Who are you—my mother? Always thinking that I'm too young to know what I'm doing? I know what I'm doing."

"We've been planning this summer adventure for months!" Jenna exclaimed. "You can't just pack up and leave. We just got here!"

"This is a free country. I can change my mind about what I want to do."

"But we're only going to be here six weeks," I reminded her. "Chad will still be there."

"I'm not going back for Chad. I'm going back for me. You don't understand how I feel about him."

I stepped in front of her, trying to stop yet another mad dash between her dresser and the suitcase on the bed. "I know you're crazy about Chad—"

"Not Chad. Sean. I really, *really* like Sean." She dropped down on the bed, scrunching her clothes between her hands. "That first night when we were listening to the band at that bar, I was leaning into him and he had his arm around me, and I wasn't thinking about Chad at all. I was just thinking about how nice it was to be with Sean. And then yesterday at the swamp—I knew I should have been hanging around with you."

"What could you do? He took your hand—"

"He took my hand because he thinks I really like him. He doesn't even know about Chad."

"He doesn't know you have a boyfriend?"

"How do you tell a guy that?"

"'Oh, by the way, I have a boyfriend?'"

"But what if I shouldn't?"

"What?" Jenna asked, while I said, "Huh?"

I was afraid Amber was about to veer off into one of her strange thoughts that we couldn't follow.

"Look—Chad? He's the only one I've ever wanted to date. I've been crushing on him since I was a freshman. When he finally asked me out over winter break, I thought he was it. Forever. And now, all of a sudden, it's like all I can think about is Sean. And that's so wrong. I know it's wrong. He's like that extra scoop of ice cream that you know you shouldn't have, but you can't resist it. I need to get as far away from the ice cream as possible. I need to go home."

Okay, some of what she was saying was making sense. I wanted to try to convince her that she should stay, but I couldn't anymore. I couldn't without fearing that she'd cheat on Chad—and I'd be encouraging it. She was right. It was better to leave and figure out what was going on.

"I know if we hadn't gone to see the psychic that I wouldn't have all these doubts. Or maybe I would. I just don't know anymore. I mean, what was I thinking to even consider going away for most of the summer? I have a boyfriend and nothing should be more important than him."

Jenna sat on the edge of the bed and drew her long legs up beneath her. "You know, what you're doing is sort of self-fulfilling Sara's prophecy. You're going to make happen exactly what she predicted. Just like Tank was talking about."

"You can't tell me that you weren't a little freaked out when you saw that tattoo."

"I was surprised," Jenna admitted. "But it could be that we're taking her words and seeing things that apply. We're assuming she meant the tattoo because it fits. But it could mean something else."

"Like what?" Amber challenged.

Jenna sighed. "I don't know."

Okay. I thought it was a little difficult to read anything else into that tattoo, but I understood what Jenna was saying—or trying to say. You see what you expect to see, and Saraphina had influenced what we expected to see.

Amber turned to me. "Look at the bright side. You don't have to sleep on the AeroBed anymore. You can have a real bed."

"The bed isn't an issue. I'd rather have you here."

"I can't, guys. I'm sorry, but I just can't stay."

An hour later, Jenna and I hugged Amber good-bye and watched her climb into the minivan. Ms. Wynder, after repeatedly clucking about how sorry she was that Amber's grandmother had died, drove Amber to the airport where she could catch her flight back to Houston.

"Whose idea was it to visit the psychic, anyway?" Jenna asked as we trudged back to our room.

"I think it was Amber's."

"Talk about a fun idea going bad."

"It is a little . . . eerie, though."

"Yeah, but at least I didn't see the tattoo until after I'd fallen for Tank, so my feelings about him are my own. Do you ever worry that what you feel for Brady is because of the reading? I mean, would you have noticed him if you hadn't been looking for a red Chiefs cap?"

"I wasn't looking for a red Chiefs cap."

"Okay, you weren't looking, but when you saw it—I saw your jaw drop, so I know he caught your attention. Would you have noticed him without the reading?"

"Yeah, I think I would have." I sighed. "But I might not have shot up my defenses so fast. Or maybe I would have. I don't know, Jenna. I just really don't want a guy in my life right now."

"At least you're not totally avoiding him and flying back home."

"That would be a bit extreme, especially since I really do want to be *here*."

Jenna smiled at me. I gave her a weary smile back. To say I was exhausted was an understatement. We'd worked harder and longer today than yesterday. On top of that, dealing with Amber's hysterics—

"Dibs on the shower," I muttered.

I wanted the shower first, last, and always. It felt so wonderful to get all the grit and grime off. Amber had hit the shower as soon as we'd gotten back to the room. When she'd come out, she'd gone immediately into frantic I've-got-to-get-out-of-here mode. And Jenna and I had gone into intervention mode. A lot of good that had done.

I guess, being alone with her thoughts, Amber hadn't liked where she and Sean were going.

I was too tired to think of anything except how great the shower felt. And if Jenna wasn't a friend, I probably wouldn't have cared about using up all the hot water.

The bathroom was steamy by the time I was finished; the mirror fogged. Not that I needed a mirror when I only planned to comb the tangles out my hair. When that was done, I massaged my peach-scented body lotion on my legs, arms, and hands. I'd picked up a few scratches on my arms, even though I'd tried to be careful. But nothing serious.

I slipped on cotton boxers and a tank. I was ready to fall into bed and fall asleep.

When I opened the bathroom door, the only light in the room came from the bathroom behind me.

Jenna rolled off her bed and walked toward me, holding her cell phone out. "Here."

"What's that?"

"Phone."

"I know that. I mean, who is it?"

"Brady."

"You were talking to Brady?"

"No, I was talking to Tank, but Brady wanted to talk to you when you finally got out of the bathroom. Did you even leave me any hot water?" She took my hand and wrapped my fingers around her phone. "He doesn't have your phone number. Keep talking until I'm finished with my shower."

She closed the door, leaving me in the dark except for the phone's little bit of indigo glow. I stumbled to the bed, sat down, and stared at the phone for a minute like it was the snake that had slithered out from beneath one of the boards we'd moved that afternoon. Some guy had used a shovel to kill it, and we'd all heard a lecture from Sara about how we should live in harmony with all creatures. The dead snake had upset her. Personally I didn't have a problem with killing anything that slithered and stuck its tongue out at me.

And why did I have to talk to Brady until Jenna got out of the bathroom? It wasn't like she didn't already have Tank's number programmed into her phone, so she could call him back. What about *I really don't want to get involved with anyone this summer* did she not understand?

I moved the phone to my ear. "Hello?"

"Hey."

His voice was as sultry as the Louisiana night. I could almost hear the crickets chirping and the bullfrogs croaking in a bayou. Oh, wait. That could have been them outside the dorm window, since quite a bit of water surrounded the Crescent City.

"You okay?" he asked. "You sound kinda dazed."

"Nah, just totally relaxed after a hot shower."

Which suddenly seemed like a really personal thing to say to him. Maybe he was thinking the same thing, because he didn't say anything. It was definitely a conversation stopper.

"So, uh, Jenna said you wanted to talk to me?"

"Yeah. I, uh . . . this is awkward."

"What?"

"Well, Sean said that Amber's heading home because she has a boyfriend."

"How does he know that?"

"She called him from the airport. Upset. It was strange."

I imagined it was. But Amber was my friend. I wasn't going to call her strange.

"Well, anyway," Brady continued, "I just—it's just that I didn't even think to ask, but do *you* have a boyfriend?"

My heart thudded, because why would he ask unless he was interested? Who was I kidding? He'd kissed me. And we'd hung out a little.

All I had to do was say yes, and he'd move

on. Instead, I heard myself telling him the truth. "No."

"Okay."

What did that mean? I wished we were talking face to face so I could see what he was thinking.

The silence stretched out between us. Finally I couldn't take it anymore.

"Okay?" I repeated. "What do you mean by that?"

"Just okay. Now I know you don't have a boyfriend."

"Do you have a girlfriend?"

"Why do you care?"

"I don't," I responded quickly. I felt like I'd been tricked into revealing something, but I didn't know what. "I mean why would I care? We're just here for the summer, working, having a little fun."

"Okay."

"Okay."

But I felt like something had shifted, and I wasn't sure what.

The door opened. Mist, light, and the scent

of strawberry shower gel wafted out.

"Jenna's ready to take back her phone," I said, hating that I sounded so relieved. Hating even more that I wasn't relieved at all. Should I give him my number? Should I ask for his? Did I even want to continue this conversation?

"See you tomorrow," Brady said.

"Yeah."

I held the phone out to Jenna. "Thanks."

She took the phone, reached back, and turned out the bathroom light. She was whispering quietly as she crawled into bed.

I slipped beneath the sheet and blankets. We'd turned the thermostat on the air conditioner way down and now that I didn't have Brady's voice to keep me warm, I was feeling the chill of the room.

Maybe it was because I was sleeping in the bed that Amber had been sleeping in, but I kept thinking about her telling me that I needed to climb back in the saddle. And I kept thinking of climbing in the saddle with Brady.

Because it was going to be a very long and

lonely summer if I didn't take some action. Now that Amber was gone and Jenna was practically glued to Tank, I was going to be spending a lot of time alone. Unless I wanted to hang out with Ms. Wynder. And I wasn't sure that was even an option because I'd seen her near the porta-potties laughing with John. And no one laughs near porta-potties, so I had a feeling something was going on there.

Suddenly I realized that it was really quiet in the room. That I couldn't hear Jenna whispering anymore. I heard her bed creak as she shifted on it.

"Dawn?" she whispered.

"Yeah."

"You still awake?"

I smiled in the dark. "Nah, I'm talking in my sleep."

She released a small laugh. "You're so funny."

No, not usually.

"Listen," she began, "in the morning I'm going to go have breakfast with Tank at Café Du Monde. Wanna come? It's one of those places you should eat at once in your life."

"Did Tank tell you that?"

"No, actually, my dad told me that he wanted me to eat there. He said Jimmy Buffett mentions it in one of his songs and Dad's a huge Jimmy Buffett fan, so he told me to go eat some beignets on him." She laughed. "Actually everything I eat is on him since he's the one who gave me the money for this trip. So, anyway, do you want to come?"

"Is it going to be just you and Tank?" Not that her answer should really affect my decision but still—

"No, Brady will be there for sure. Maybe Sean. So what do you think?"

I rolled onto my side. I couldn't really see her because of the darkness, but it made it easier to talk to her. "Jenna, if I keep doing stuff with him, he's going to think I'm interested."

"I'm going to keep seeing Tank."

It wasn't like Jenna to be this determined.

"But I want to spend time with you, too," she said. "I'm just talking about you going to get a doughnut with *us*. So what if Brady is there? Big deal."

"I thought it was a beignet."

"Beignet, doughnut — same thing. We wanted to have fun this summer, didn't we?"

Yeah, we did. We'd wanted to do some good, but we'd also wanted some adventure, some laughs, some memories. It was our first summer away from home. Where was my adventuresome spirit?

"Okay," I said. "Yeah, I'm in. Totally."

She didn't take offense that I sounded resigned instead of overjoyed. She just said, "Great."

Yeah, I thought, as I rolled back over and closed my eyes.

Great.

Chapter 11

I'd expected to sleep like a rock, or a log, or something heavy and inanimate. Instead I woke up while it was still dark and couldn't go back to sleep.

I crawled out of bed, grabbed my clothes from the chair where I'd left them the night before, and crept into the bathroom. Once I closed the door, I turned on the light and got dressed as quietly as I could. Today I was going to wear coveralls over a tube top. Coveralls had seemed like a building-house-kinda-thing to wear, but now I was wondering if maybe they'd be too hot. At least my shoulders would be cool.

And bare. Maybe a little sexy.

Oh no, I was thinking about Brady again. I

didn't want to do things to get his attention.

I don't know how long I sat on the edge of the tub and worried about how I could spend time with Jenna, without getting in over my head with Brady. A sudden rap on the door startled me. I nearly fell backward into the tub. Just what I needed—to start the day with a concussion.

"You okay in there?" Jenna asked.

"Oh yeah, I'm fine." I got up and opened the door. "I couldn't sleep and I didn't want to wake you."

She yawned. "Ow. I can barely move this morning. Working with a crowbar was harder work than I thought."

She stumbled into the bathroom as I walked out.

"Call Ms. Wynder and tell her we're going to breakfast with some friends," she said before shutting the door.

"You think she's up?" I called through the door.

"Oh yeah."

I called Ms. Wynder. She was indeed up,

sounding way too bright and cheery for that time of day. She said she was fine with us doing breakfast elsewhere, and she'd see us at the site.

When Jenna came out of the bathroom, we grabbed our backpacks and headed outside.

The dorm was a square, uninteresting brick building, part of a campus that had survived the storm. It was early morning but humidity already hung heavy in the air.

Parked at the front of the drive, in a no-parking zone, was the black Civic. Our two guys were leaning against it—one against the hood, one against the trunk—arms crossed over their chests. Totally sexy pose. Rebels, I thought, and my heart did a little stutter. What was I getting myself into?

"Hey," Tank said as we got nearer.

"Hey, yourself," Jenna said, practically skipping to his side.

He grinned at her. No kiss. No hug. But it seemed to be enough for her as she slid into the front passenger seat, and it probably was. After all, he hadn't tattooed her name on his arm yet. I suddenly wondered if he would someday.

Then I wondered if maybe that was where I'd made my mistake. I always wanted things to happen fast. Drew and I were a steady item after that first date. I'd never questioned where the relationship was going; I'd just followed where it had seemed to lead. Now I was trying to question everything.

Brady just grinned at me, tapped the brim of my "Life Is Good" cap. "You ever not wear that thing?" he asked.

I touched the brim of his. "Same goes."

"Yeah, but I use mine to hide a bald spot. You got a bald spot under there that I need to know about?"

"No. Do you? I mean really? Bald?"

He laughed. "Nah. At least not yet. Someday. If I take after my dad."

"I think bald men are sexy."

I don't know what made me say that.

"Really?" he asked, opening the door to the backseat.

"Really." I climbed inside, scooted across, and he got in.

"Like who?" he asked. "Give me a name."

"Bruce Willis."

"Is he shaved or bald?"

"Is there a difference?"

"Oh yeah. Shaved you have a choice. Bald you don't."

"How bald is your dad?" I asked.

"Pretty bald."

"Bet he's pretty sexy."

"Yeah, and what do you base that assumption on?" His grin was cocky, almost a dare.

And I almost responded with "you." But that would have taken the flirting to a whole new level, and I wasn't even sure that I should be flirting.

Instead I looked out the window as Tank drove along the street. "Looks like it's gonna be another scorcher today."

It was my dad's equivalent of Mom's "I think I left the iron on." A detour in the conversation.

Brady laughed and leaned back in the corner. I could feel him studying me, and I wondered what he was thinking. The easiest way to find out would be to ask. But I didn't.

♥ ♥ ♥

We couldn't find a parking spot near Café Du
Monde, so we parked several streets over and
walked. Although it was early, people were
queued up on the sidewalk. A very small portion of the restaurant was indoor seating. Most
of the seating was outdoors, some beneath a
roof, some beneath a large green-and-white
striped canopy.

As we waited in line, Jenna was nestled
against Tank's side, and they were doing that
quiet talking thing they did. I couldn't figure
out how two such tall people could talk so quietly. And Tank wasn't only tall, he was broad.
He was wearing a tank top today and the muscles of his arms rippled and when they did, so
did the dragon on his shoulder that was peering
out beneath his shirt.

"Like his ink?" Brady asked.

"Oh, gosh, I was staring, wasn't I? That
was rude."

He shrugged. "It's an unusual piece. He
goes to a guy who does original artwork, so
nothing he's ever tattooed on anyone has ever

been put on anyone else."

"That's cool. I've never heard of that. I thought you just looked in a catalogue and picked out the one you wanted."

"You can do it that way. But Tank—he never follows the crowd."

"Do you have any tattoos?" Was that question too personal? If he did, they were well hidden because I hadn't noticed any the couple of times I'd seen him without his shirt.

Brady shook his head. "Nah. Been thinking about it, but I don't know if there's anything I'd want forever. I mean, how do I know I won't change my mind? How 'bout you?"

"I did a temporary one once. A peel-on wash-off."

He grinned. "How did that work for you?"

"Not too bad, except I got it out of a machine, like a bubblegum machine, and so I just had to take what it dispensed. It was a skull with a snake coming out of the eye socket. Gross. But I was fourteen, and for a quarter, it was a great deal."

"Where'd you put it?"

"On my wrist."

He looked disappointed, like maybe he'd been fantasizing about it being someplace really personal. And that made me feel very unadventuresome.

"Hey, I had to put it someplace I could reach," I explained.

"Very unimaginative," he said. "Next time you want a tat, I'll help you put it someplace you can't reach."

I narrowed my eyes. "Like where?"

"Your hip, maybe. Someplace so it just peeks out over the waistband of your jeans."

I got warm just *thinking* about him applying the tattoo. I couldn't imagine what would happen if he was actually putting it on. I really wanted—needed—to talk about something else.

"So where's Sean?"

"He hooked up with Sara."

I stared at him. "The psychic?"

Brady grinned. "Yeah. Is that a problem?"

"No, I just"—I shivered—"I don't know if I'd want to be involved with someone who could read my mind."

"Do psychics read minds?" he asked.

"I don't know. They read something. All that paranormal stuff just seems to mesh together. I don't know if there's a line that distinguishes what a person can or can't do."

"She seems nice anyway."

"Oh, well, yeah. I mean, she doesn't seem evil or anything." Then something else occurred to me. I scoffed and muttered, "She didn't have to leave."

"Huh?"

"Amber—she, well, she didn't have to leave. If she'd known Sean was interested in Sara—"

"I don't think he was interested. He was just bummed out because Amber left, so we hit some bars last night." He shrugged. "Sara was at one of them."

"Oh."

So had he turned to Sara because he'd been heartbroken? That made me sad. Why did love—or even just liking someone—have to be so complicated?

We finally got to the front of the line. It was an unorganized type of organization, and

I wasn't at all sure how the staff remembered who had been waited on and who hadn't.

As soon as people got up from a table, people sat down at it—mess and all. Then the server would come clean up the mess, take the order, and head over to another table and do the same thing.

"Over here," Tank said and led us to a just-vacated table.

It was covered in plates, cups, and loads of powdered sugar. We dusted off the chairs before sitting down.

"This is something that just has to be experienced to be believed," Tank said.

The server came over and began clearing the table. "Order?"

"Two orders of beignets and four café au laits," Tank said. Then looked around at us. "Any objections?"

"Sounds good," I said.

Jenna just smiled.

"We're going to be sticky after this, aren't we?" I asked.

"Oh yeah," Tank said. "But it's worth it."

I couldn't believe how crowded it was. And how fast the servers were taking care of people. Apparently Café Du Monde was a tradition for tourists and locals alike.

The waiter brought over our two plates of the little fried squares of dough smothered in confectioners' sugar. He also set down our mugs of café au lait—half coffee, half milk. It all smelled really good.

I picked up a beignet. It was still hot, very hot, just out of the fryer, and the powdered sugar floated around me. There was a jar of more sugar on the table. Not that I could imagine anyone ever needing to add any to the beignets. I bit into the fried dough. Was it ever good!

We made an absolute mess as we ate, leaving powdered sugar all over our faces, our hands, our clothes, but no one seemed to mind.

I kept sneaking peeks at Brady, only to discover him looking at me. It was starting to get awkward. I was afraid I was sending a message I didn't want to send, like that I was obsessed with him or something—when I wasn't. I wasn't going to let myself be.

Even though it seemed like he might be interested in me. Sean had tried to hook up with Amber, and then he'd hooked up with Sara. While Brady, as far as I know, hadn't tried to get together with anyone except me.

So was he interested?

I was pretty sure he was, but he was keeping it cool. Casual. I thought maybe I could handle that.

Maybe.

Chapter 12

"I'm sorry your friend left," Saraphina—oops, she was Sara when she wasn't at the shop— said.

I was in the backyard, sawing off the dead branches of an uprooted tree. The tree itself was dead as well, rotting, and nothing more than an eyesore. But it was also huge. I could imagine the wondrous shade that it had provided for the nearby house. I could certainly use some shade now. It was late morning, and we were waiting for the truck with the lumber and supplies to arrive, filling in the time with odd jobs.

"She just got a little freaked," I explained.

"Sometimes people do that," Sara said, picking up scattered smaller branches and tossing them into the wheelbarrow.

I stopped sawing for a moment and took the red bandanna Brady had given me earlier and wiped my brow. When he'd given it to me, it had been wet and cold and he'd wrapped it around my neck to help cool me down. It had felt so good that I hadn't even been bothered that it was such a boyfriend kind of thing to do. Now all the water had evaporated, and I was using it as a towel to mop my face.

"How long have you been able to see things?" I asked.

"As long as I can remember."

"Do you see your own future?" I thought that would be pretty weird. Would you know what days not to get out of bed?

Hmm. That might be advantageous.

"I see things, but I don't always know who they apply to. Sometimes the visions are stronger when I'm touching someone, but it doesn't necessarily mean it's for that person. It's hard to explain."

"But the things you predicted, they've all sort of happened."

"Sometimes I get them right."

"Do you like being psychic?"

"It has its moments."

"Have you ever helped the police?"

She laughed. "At least you don't think it's a parlor trick. I tried to help them once, but they're as skeptical as your friend was."

I placed the saw on the branch and started moving it back and forth. "I think she's an actual believer now."

"She'll be back here before the end of summer," Sara said quietly.

I stilled the saw and looked over my shoulder at Sara.

She shrugged. "I see her here, but all this looks less messy."

"I didn't think you gave free readings."

"This isn't really a reading. It's just conversation."

But that didn't make it any less spooky.

"Is she just visiting or coming to help?" I asked.

"That I can't say."

"You can't or you won't?"

She smiled. "I don't know why she's here. I only know that she's here. And I see someone else . . . a guy with black hair. I see things getting broken."

Chad had black hair, but how could things get broken if he was here with her? That meant everything was fixed. Didn't it?

"What exactly does that mean?" I asked.

Again, she shook her head.

"I know, I know. You can tell me only what you see, not what it means. You must have been wildly popular at sleepovers."

She laughed. She had a light, lyrical laugh. It seemed to suit her.

Reaching out, she wrapped her hand around mine. "Don't be afraid to rebuild."

I started sawing diligently. "Does this look like I'm afraid?"

"No, Dawn, it doesn't. But looks are often deceiving."

"No offense, but I'd like to have a conversation with you sometime when you didn't tell me the things you were seeing."

"That would be nice. Normal, even," she said, smiling.

"Have you ever seen the endings of movies

that you're watching?" Jenna asked as she walked over and handed each of us a bottle of water. "That would be a total bummer."

She'd missed the rest of our conversation, having gone on another water run. We were trying to drink as much as we could. One girl had fainted yesterday. They called EMTs who had taken her to the hospital. She was going to be fine, but it was a reminder that we needed lots of fluids throughout the day.

"No," Sara said. "And I don't know any winning lottery numbers or who's going to win the Super Bowl. I can't control what I see. It just happens. Anyway, I didn't come over here to discuss my visions. I'm organizing a group to go on a ghost tour Saturday night, and I wanted to see if you were interested in coming."

"That would be fun," I said. I looked at Jenna to gauge her reaction and knew what she was going to say before she said it. Sara's psychic ability was rubbing off on me.

"I'm sort of leaving Saturday night free for now, in case something . . . well, maybe you already know. Am I going to have other plans?"

"No, you won't have other plans."

"Oh." Jenna's face fell. "Then I guess I'll say yes."

"She could be wrong," I told Jenna. "Not everything she sees is an absolute."

"This is," Sara said smugly.

"So you saw her on the ghost tour?"

"No, Tank told me that he and Jenna were coming. So I was just asking you, Dawn, because I figured Jenna's answer was already yes. Are you interested?"

Was I, or did I want to keep Saturday night open? Open for what? A better offer? I wasn't looking for a date. So what could be better than getting up close and personal with ghosts?

"Sounds like fun," I said. "I'm definitely there."

"Good. We'll meet outside my shop at nine." She turned to walk away, then stopped. "And just so you know—I'll be matching people up into pairs. You'll be with Brady."

"He's going to be there?"

She gave me a secretive smile. "I'm pretty sure he is. He asked if you were going, so I just assumed . . ."

Her voice trailed off. I wasn't sure I liked

what she was assuming.

"What if I'd said no?" I asked her.

"I knew you wouldn't."

"How did you know?"

She smiled all-knowingly. "Because I'm a psychic."

She could be really irritating, but I liked her.

She walked away, humming a song that sounded strangely like the theme from *Ghostbusters*. Sometimes I didn't know whether to take her seriously. But how could I not?

"She gives me the creeps," Jenna said, picking up branches and tossing them into the wheelbarrow. "I don't care how nice she is, she gives me the creeps. She just knows too much."

"At least we have something to do Saturday night."

"Are you okay with having a date?"

"It's only a date if he asks, and he didn't," I pointed out.

Jenna held up her hands. "Okay, I guess. It's not a date."

Still, it felt like maybe it was.

And if it was, could I get hurt?

♥ ♥ ♥

"Ow!"

"Hold still," Brady commanded—like a drill sergeant or something—as he studied my palm and the large sliver of wood that had slid under my skin.

"You're not the boss of me," I grumbled.

He looked up and grinned. "That's real mature. I thought only guys were bad patients."

Just before noon, lumber had been delivered on a long-bed truck. We'd been unloading it, carrying it into the yard, and stacking it up. Brady had been there helping me.

We'd been carrying some boards across the yard when I'd tripped and lost my balance. I'd landed hard, and in trying to not drop the wood, I'd ended up with a wickedly long splinter.

I should have been wearing my gloves. But they were hot, making my hands all sweaty, and I was tired of being hot and sweaty. Stupid, I know. But I'd thought I'd be okay. They'd told us we didn't need to wear our hard hats or goggles while unloading the truck.

It didn't make me feel any better that Brady

had wrapped his hand around my arm and hauled me across the front yard. He'd grabbed the first-aid kit from Sara and then led me to a picnic table where the blueprints for the house had been spread out earlier. He'd set the first-aid kit down. Then he'd put his hands on my waist, picked me up, and set me on the table—like I couldn't have gotten up there by myself.

I didn't even know why I had to be sitting down. I wasn't going to faint. I could probably take out the splinter myself.

I knew I shouldn't be irritated, but I was.

"About Saturday night," I said.

He looked up again from studying my hand. I didn't think even a palm reader would look at a hand that much.

"The ghost tour? It's not a date," I told him.

"Okay. I didn't think it was."

"You didn't?"

"Nope."

"But you asked if I was going to be there."

He shrugged—like that was an answer. I suddenly felt bad for being snappish and was worried that I might have hurt his feelings.

"Look, don't take it personally. I'm just not dating this summer."

He studied me for a minute, then said, "Okay."

"I mean, you're nice and all—"

"Nice *and all*? Please. You're going to make me blush with the compliments."

I scowled. "You know what I mean."

"Actually I don't. What's included in 'all'?"

Terrific smile, great shoulders, strong arms—

I shook my head. "You're missing the important part of what I'm trying to say here."

"You're not dating."

"Right."

"But if I get scared on the ghost tour, can I hold your hand?"

I stared at him a minute. Was he teasing? "You're going to get scared?"

"I could. Ghosts. They're frightening." He rolled his amazing shoulders dramatically. "I get goose bumps just thinking about them."

"Do you believe in ghosts?"

"Oh yeah. Especially when they help me get babes."

I smiled. Did he take anything seriously? Other than a splinter in my hand. That he seemed to take way too seriously.

"You don't believe in ghosts," I said.

"Hey, I believed in Santa Claus until I was seventeen."

"Really?"

"My mom told me if I stopped believing, no more presents on Christmas morning. So, yeah. I believed."

"Why stop at seventeen?"

"Got tired of getting toy fire trucks."

I laughed.

He opened the first-aid kit and took out a pair of tweezers. They looked so tiny in his large hand. Had I ever noticed how large his hands were? How tanned? How steady? How strong?

Was I suddenly developing a hand fetish?

"Do you even know what you're doing?" I asked.

He furrowed his brow. Suddenly he seemed

to realize something. He jerked off his sunglasses and hooked them in the front of my coveralls.

"No wonder I couldn't see," he said.

He spread my palm wide, shifted around so he wasn't creating a shadow over my hand.

"It's really in there," he said.

"Let me look."

"I've got it, but this is probably going to hurt."

No surprise there. It did.

But as far as hurts go, it wasn't too bad. And I couldn't help but be relieved. I'd been careless. I'd gotten hurt. Just like Sara had predicted. And that irritated me, too. Even knowing the future, I hadn't been able to change it.

Brady poured alcohol over my palm.

"Ow!" I jerked my hand free and waved it in the air to get the stuff to evaporate.

"Sorry." Then he laughed. "You're such a baby."

"Am not."

"Are to." He moved near, put his hands on my waist, and leaned in. "But that's okay.

Because I have a thing for babes."

I thought he was going to kiss me, but he just lifted me off the table.

"Be careful. I don't like it when you get hurt," he said.

"You think I do?"

I stepped away, thinking I might get hurt again—worse—if I stayed close to him. I handed him his sunglasses. We took the first-aid kit back to Sara.

"You okay?" she asked me.

"Oh yeah, just a little hurt." I smiled. "Which you predicted."

"I predicted a splinter?"

"You predicted I'd be careless and get hurt."

She furrowed her brow and a faraway look came into her eyes.

Oh God, maybe the splinter wasn't the hurt. It probably wasn't. It couldn't be that simple.

"Whatever it is," I said hastily, "I don't want to know. Thanks just the same."

I started walking away, and Brady hurried to catch up.

"Hey, that was kinda rude," he said.

"I really don't want to know what she sees. She says things like they're all innocent, but—" I shook my head. "I just really don't want to know."

That night John arranged for us to have reserved tables at a local restaurant and club— for crawfish étouffée and blues music. The blues originated in the African-American community. To me, it sounded as though the notes themselves were melancholy.

As soon as we walked into the restaurant, he snagged Ms. Wynder and led her over to his table. A table for two away from everyone else.

Jenna waved at someone, and I didn't need to look around her to know who she was waving at. I was slightly disappointed when we got to the table to discover it was a small one, with only four chairs. Tank and Brady were sitting in two of them.

Jenna sat beside Tank, then looked at me as if it was a foregone conclusion I'd sit between her and Brady, so I sat. And then wondered if I should have asked Brady if it was okay.

"John reminds me of a cruise director," Jenna said. "Making sure everyone has something to do."

Tank nodded. "That's one of the great things about volunteering here in New Orleans. You can work during the day, but party at night. The tourist part of voluntourism. And the businesses here need the tourist dollars as much as the people need help getting their homes rebuilt."

Then he leaned toward Jenna and they started that low talking that they did. Drew and I hadn't whispered that much to each other in the entire year and a half that we were together.

Don't compare them to you and Drew, I scolded myself. *Just don't.*

Because they were nothing like us. I didn't want them to be anything like us. But in a way they were. When Jenna was with Tank, he was all that mattered to her.

Just the thought of ever feeling that way again made me nervous.

On John's recommendation, we all ordered

the étouffée, a spicy Cajun stew served over rice. Cajuns were descendents of Acadian exiles—French Canadians. Their influence was strong in the city.

"I think John has a thing for your chaperone," Brady said.

He was leaning near so I could hear him over the music being played. His breath wafted over my ear. It sent a shiver, a very nice shiver, down my back.

I looked at him and smiled. "She's not really our chaperone, she's more like our sponsor, I guess."

"Sponsor? Makes it sound like you're in a rehab program."

"No, I'm in a cleaning-up-New-Orleans program." I tapped the table, trying to decide if I should give him the option of having someone else sit here. Was it fair to him for me to take a seat beside him when I wasn't going to spend the night whispering low?

"Listen—"

"You're not wearing your Life Is Good hat," he said. "Is life suddenly not good?"

"What? Oh." I touched my head, as though I needed to verify that I hadn't worn it. I usually tucked it into a pocket so I could put it on as soon as I took off my hard hat. But tonight I'd clipped my hair back.

"No. Life is great. I don't *always* wear it. You're not wearing your hat."

"True."

And his hair kept falling forward. I wanted to reach out and brush it back.

"So you're sitting here," he said. "Coincidence or intentional?"

That was a hard one.

"It had to be intentional; I mean, I didn't just discover the chair beneath my butt."

He smiled. So maybe I was going to get off easy, without having to actually explain anything about what I was feeling.

"You said you're not dating this summer," he said.

Okay, maybe I was going to have to explain after all. "Right. I'm planning on this being a dateless summer."

"Dateless summer? Wasn't that a movie?"

"You're thinking of *The Endless Summer*."

"A summer without a date would seem pretty endless—or at least it would to me."

I smiled again. And maybe he even had a point. I didn't want to think too much about that.

"The movie was about surfing," I said.

"So we're really talking about the movie here?"

No, we weren't, but it was a more comfortable topic than my whole not-dating thing. Before I could say anything else, he said, "You don't have a boyfriend."

"No."

"So is there someone you're interested in?"

Was he hoping I'd say him? I swallowed hard. This was so hard to say, embarrassing even. "Look, there *was* a boyfriend."

He studied me for a minute and finally asked, "Bad breakup?"

I nodded.

"When?"

"About six weeks ago."

"Okay."

"What do you mean okay?"

"I get it now."

"What's to get?"

"You don't want to date. And I'm okay with that. I don't want to date either."

"Really?" Was I relieved or actually a little hurt? Yes, I think I was—hurt.

"Look, just because you don't want to date, and I don't want to date, that doesn't mean I wouldn't like to hang out," he said. "Or even that we couldn't hang out. I mean, look around. Everyone's pretty much paired up already."

I did take the time to look around then. Yeah, I could see what he meant.

"So, you're saying we're kinda stuck with each other?" I asked.

"Is that such a bad thing? You're fun. I'm fun. We could double our fun."

"You had better pickup lines the other night."

He grinned. "Yeah, but this isn't a pick-up." He shook his head. "I'm not sure what this is. Maybe just trying to define what we've got going on here."

What was going on? A casual romance? A summer fling? Summer buddies?

Tonight my thoughts were being influenced by the blues. The thrill definitely wasn't gone. It was fun to have someone to share things with, and Jenna was clearly no longer available.

So I could hang out with Brady. Nothing serious. Nothing permanent. At the end of the six weeks, we'd each go our separate ways. And in the meantime, we'd have fun.

And wasn't that the reason I was here?

I mean, besides helping to rebuild, I wanted to have a great summer.

"I'm not looking for anything serious," I told him.

"Not a problem. I know a thousand knock-knock jokes."

I smiled. "Seriously—"

"Didn't think you wanted serious."

"Look, nothing long-term. Just a New Orleans thing," I said.

"Okay."

I moved closer to him and moved my shoulders in rhythm to the music.

"Then while I'm here in the Big Easy, only while I'm here"—I bobbed my head to the rhythm and blues—"we could hang out together. A friends-with-benefits kind of thing. The benefits being"—I couldn't believe I was being this bold, but if he wanted the relationship defined, I wanted to make sure we were using the same dictionary—"occasional kissing."

That really nice smile of his spread across his face. Reaching out, he wrapped his large hand around my neck and brought me nearer. "I'm good with that. Definitely good."

And then he kissed me.

Yeah, definitely good.

Chapter 13

"So . . . you and Brady," Jenna said quietly later that night as we were lying in the dark.

"Yeah. Me and Brady." I went to sleep smiling.

The next morning I woke up feeling . . . good. Really, really good. Great, in fact, not only in body but in spirit.

Some of the soreness and stiffness had finally worked its way out of my muscles, mostly I think because Brady and I did a lot of dancing the night before. Dancing to the blues. Although it hadn't really been any kind of dancing I'd done before. We'd just moved with the music and had a great time.

I'd always thought the blues meant depressing music, music determined to make you blue, but I'd been happier last night than I'd been in a long time. Being with Brady was a lot of fun. He didn't seem to take anything seriously, and that was what I needed right now. Someone who lived in the moment, someone who was all about fun.

He laughed a lot. He was always smiling. He was nothing at all like Drew. I decided Drew had been a downer. I wasn't certain what I'd ever seen in him.

I thought I actually might be on my way to recovery. And I was loving it.

I'd just pulled on jeans and was working my way into a ratty T-shirt—one I normally wore on laundry day, but decided I should wear for work because who did I want to impress anyway? Brady was already impressed—when my cell phone rang.

I snatched it up, looked at the number, and answered. "Hey, Amber."

Jenna looked up from tying her shoes, a question in her eyes.

"How's it going?" I asked Amber.

"Awesome! I wanted you guys to know that I panicked for no reason. Everything is totally cool between me and Chad. I feel like such a dummy for worrying."

"I'm glad everything's okay."

Jenna rolled her eyes and went back to tying her shoes.

"Things between us are stronger than ever. I just love him so much."

"Great." I didn't see any reason to remind her that the psychic hadn't questioned Amber's current boyfriend. She'd simply said that in college she'd find something better. Of course, that didn't meant she wouldn't find it with Chad. He could be even better as he got older. Or they could break up and another guy would be in Amber's life. Who knew?

"So what's happening with you guys?" Amber asked.

I filled her in on the fact that Jenna was definitely with Tank and I was sort of with Brady.

"Any chance I could borrow your AeroBed if I decide to head on back to New Orleans?" Amber asked.

My knees grew weak and I sat on the edge of the bed. Would Amber freak if I told her that

Saraphina had seen her back here? Yes, she'd definitely freak.

"Absolutely," I said, pushing past my own discomfort with the fact that Sara could, in fact, see into our lives. "Are you going to come back?"

"I'm thinking about it. Next week maybe. Or the week after. I don't know for sure. I was telling Chad about how satisfying it was and how it made me feel good, so he's sort of interested in maybe coming with me. I mean, we haven't worked out all the details. But he has a car, so he'd drive us. I don't know if we'd stay the whole summer, but maybe a couple of weeks. A couple of weeks are better than nothing, right?"

"A couple of weeks would be awesome," I told her. "Every little bit helps."

"Are y'all to the fun stuff yet?"

"What fun stuff? Eating, dancing, shopping?"

"The house. Aren't you going to rebuild it, decorate it?"

"We're rebuilding it. I don't know about

the decorating part."

"If you'll measure the windows, I'll sew some curtains before I come back."

Amber was the only person I knew who could—and loved to—use a sewing machine.

"That'd be great. I'll see if I can get that information for you."

We talked a little more and then I said good-bye.

"What information do you need to get?" Jenna asked, slipping on her backpack.

"Measurements for the windows. She wants to make curtains."

"She's feeling guilty."

"Probably. Although maybe she's just embarrassed that she totally overreacted to the psychic reading."

"Could be. So things are okay with her and Chad?"

"Apparently. The whole breaking up was a false alarm."

"We'll see what happens when she goes off to college," Jenna said. "Although we probably shouldn't point that out to her. She might not apply to any colleges."

"You want to know something freaky? Yesterday Sara told me that Amber would be coming back."

"You're kidding?"

I shook my head.

"Wow."

"Yeah. I didn't tell Amber, though, because her reaction to the other prediction was so out of control."

"Unlike ours. I mean, we took it in stride, right?"

I grabbed my backpack. Had I taken it in stride?

"Well, at least we don't have to worry anymore. All the predictions have been met," I said.

"Have they? Or do we just think they have?"

Goose bumps rose on my skin.

"Is there a statute of limitations on how long after a reading something will happen?" I asked.

"I don't know. Could check with Sara."

"Nah, I'm sure we're in the clear."

And checking with her might result in her having another vision. I'd definitely become a firm believer that seeing the future wasn't all that it was cracked up to be.

It's just a fact that hard-working guys are sexy. Incredibly so. Especially when the afternoon sun beat down unmercifully and they decided it was time to ditch the shirts.

Oh yeah.

It was funny in a way, because when the guys started heading to their cars, the girls stopped hammering. It was like we took a collective breath, and held it, and then released an appreciative sigh. Then we all smiled at each other, a little embarrassed, maybe, and went back to work.

I couldn't believe how fast things were going up. Brady, Tank, Sean, and a couple of other guys were working on the roof. Jenna and I were rebuilding the porch flooring. We'd ripped it up earlier because it had been rotting. I discovered that hammering was an extremely cathartic experience. I just pretended every nail was Drew's tiny, little, stupid head.

Bang, bang, bang.

It was actually fun.

We still wore the hard hats and safety goggles, but we no longer wore the masks.

"Listen," Jenna said.

I stopped hammering, looked around. "For what?"

She rolled her eyes. "To me."

"Okay. What's going on?"

She sighed. "What if Tank stops liking me?"

"He's not going to stop liking you, unless he's an idiot. And if he's an idiot then you want him to stop liking you."

Bang, bang, bang.

I moved up to put the next nail in place.

"Did you just compliment me?" she asked.

"Of course."

"Did you insult him?"

"Only if he stops liking you."

"How do I stop that from happening?"

I pounded Drew's head—I mean, the nail—into the board.

"Jenna, you're worrying for nothing. He's

182

crazy about you. You've never had a boyfriend. Enjoy it."

"Did you worry when you were dating Drew?"

I gave one more nail a hard pound and sat back on my heels. Had I worried? Good question.

"No, I don't think I did."

"Do you worry about Brady?"

"No. What I have with Brady is perfect. We both agreed it's only while we're in New Orleans. It's finite. No worries."

"What if you decide that's not enough?"

"It's enough, Jenna." I started hammering again. A summer thing with Brady. That's all I wanted. It was nice and safe.

I liked nice and safe.

Chapter 14

"We should have done this days ago," Jenna said.

We were sitting in the hot tub beside the pool at the guys' hotel. It was early Friday evening, and it felt wonderful to have the heated water swirling over my aching muscles.

The hotel was a small one with a very historic feel in the French Quarter. The guys had called that morning and told us to pack bathing suits, so we could stop by before hitting the clubs. Jenna and I had changed in Tank's room while the guys had changed in Brady's room. I thought it was generous of the hotel to give them their own rooms. According to Tank, the owner was married to a cousin of a cousin or something.

I was wearing a bikini and when we'd come out of the room, Brady had wiggled his eyebrows at me and said, "Know what you need?"

"A bubblegum machine tattoo?"

And he'd laughed.

I liked making him laugh, liked watching him smile. Liked watching the way he watched me now as the water swirled around us.

"I've had enough," Jenna said and stood.

"Not me," Brady said, and his eyes held a challenge.

A challenge to me. Was I going to choose him or Jenna?

Tank had also stood up, and I wondered if maybe Jenna wanted to be alone with him.

"I want a few more minutes," I said.

"Okay. Great," Jenna said. "I'll see you in a bit."

She wrapped a towel around her waist, and Tank wrapped his arm around her. I watched as they walked off.

"He's been dying to get some time alone with her," Brady said.

I snapped my attention back to him. "Yeah, it just occurred to me that they haven't really had much of that."

We'd gone to listen to jazz last night, but it had been another group outing. Group outings were safe. I liked them.

Brady glided through the water until he was sitting by me. "But then, neither have we."

I shook my head. Probably a little jerkily. Not being alone with him had seemed like the smart thing to do. And now that I was alone with him . . . I probably shouldn't have been.

"Go out with me tonight," he said.

I stared at him for a minute. "I *am* going out with you tonight."

"No. You're going out with me, Tank, and Jenna. I'm asking you to go out with just me."

"What—you mean like a date? You said you didn't want to date."

"I said *that*?"

"Yeah. The night we had étouffée."

"Are you sure? Maybe I was talking about the fruit, date. I don't eat fruit . . . or vegetables, for that matter."

Why was he giving me a hard time about this? We had an agreement. I shoved on his shoulder. "No, you weren't talking about fruit. You were talking about dating."

"Okay, then, I changed my mind. Is that illegal?"

It could be. When the thought of it made my heart pound so hard that I thought I could die. When we were hanging out with other people, it was easy to find things to talk about—we could always talk about the people around us. If it was just us—

The thought of being with only Brady, with no buffer, no other people, was scary and thrilling. And I suddenly realized that it was something I wanted. I wanted a lot.

I took a deep breath. "Okay."

He grinned at my use of what seemed to be a word that he thought explained everything—when it really explained nothing.

"Just okay?"

I nodded. "Just okay."

We went to House of Blues. Just the two of us. Brady and me. It was in the French Quarter, close enough that we could walk. I never walked as much at home as I walked here—but I was starting to appreciate the fact that we didn't have to get into a car to go everywhere.

Especially when Brady held my hand. He'd changed into jeans and a snug black T-shirt. He looked so hot and smelled so good. And it wasn't insect repellent, this time. The guys had gotten ready in Brady's room, while Jenna and I had showered and changed in Tank's. I was wearing white shorts and a red halter-neck top. I'd left my hair down, brushing my bare shoulders.

"I think it's great that you and Brady are going on a date," Jenna had said, as she ran her fingers through her hair.

"It's not a date."

She'd looked at me, her lips pursed.

"Okay, it's a date."

"We'll meet back here in the lobby at eleven-thirty so Tank can drive us back to the dorm in time for the bed check."

"Sounds like a plan."

She'd hugged me. "Have fun."

"You, too."

"Oh, I will. Definitely."

Now Brady and I were being seated outside in the voodoo garden. My sandals clicked over the bricks as we followed the hostess to a round table covered in a blue tablecloth. A live band was playing—what else?—blues.

Whenever I thought about voodoo, I thought of scenes from shows or movies where voodoo was used for evil. But I'd learned that, like everything, it has two sides, and here was the peaceful, tranquil, bringing-everything-into-harmony side. Lots of lush, green plants surrounded us. It was simply a place that made me glad to be there.

Brady scooted his chair closer to me. "So I can see the band better," he said.

I smiled. "Yeah, right."

"Okay, so I want to be closer to you. Is that a bad thing?"

"No, it's nice, actually."

Very nice.

After dinner, he moved his chair even closer, put his arm around me, and we settled back to enjoy the music—drinking virgin daiquiris so we wouldn't get kicked out for taking space from paying customers.

It felt right. And was no longer scaring me. Or at least not scaring me as much as it had. As long as I kept everything in perspective.

When the band took a break, I said, "This hanging out that we're doing, it's only for the summer."

I needed to be sure that I wasn't expecting more than I was going to get. And that *he* wasn't expecting more than he was going to get.

"Right," Brady said. "That's what we both wanted. Just for the summer, just while we're here."

"I just want to make sure that you under-stand that it's *only* while we're in the Big Easy, even though we've sorta moved into actual dat-ing territory."

"I get it."

Did he?

"I mean, it's a set period of time. When one of us leaves New Orleans—whoever leaves first—that's it, it's over. No good-bye. Good-bye is understood."

"What? You want me to sign a contract? I

get what you're saying. And it's what I want, too. A hundred percent."

"I just don't want another breakup. I just want an 'it's over' but without either of us saying it's over."

"And you think that'll make it easier?"

"Knowing that it's coming, being prepared? Yeah, I do. We'll be together five weeks, and then that's it. We move on."

"Okay."

I released a long sigh. "Okay."

It would be easier. I was sure it would be.

He absently-mindedly traced his finger across my bare shoulders, back and forth. It felt delicious.

"Where are you going to go to college?" he asked.

"I haven't decided for sure."

"Okay."

"Why do you say that so much? Just 'okay.'"

"So you know I heard you, but don't have anything else to add." He nuzzled my neck. "And sometimes just so you know I understand."

We were in the shadows. No one was paying

any attention to us. He kissed my shoulder, and I thought I might not wear anything that covered my shoulders ever again.

"You understand a lot without me saying much," I said.

"I have three sisters who think I'm Dr. Phil. I've heard about every rotten thing that every guy they've dated has ever done to them. And they always end with, 'If you ever do that to a girl . . .'"

His voice had gone prissy at the end.

"As though I would," he finished in his normal voice.

"What would they do if you did?"

He shrugged. "They never say. But knowing them, it'd be a fate worse than death—forcing me to sit through a marathon of romantic comedies or something."

Brady had a way of always making me smile.

"Still, I bet you make a great Dr. Phil."

He pointed up. "Especially once I get the bald thing going."

I laughed. "You're really bothered about losing your hair."

"Yeah, I think I am. Vain, I guess."

I leaned into him. "You really shouldn't worry about it."

"No?"

"No."

"Okay."

Then he leaned in and kissed me. Being with him without Jenna around wasn't nearly as uncomfortable as I'd expected it to be. Actually, it seemed natural.

He told me funny stories about his sisters. Two were older, one younger, and he finally admitted that he was offended that they'd think he'd ever do any of the jerk stuff guys had pulled on them.

"Why can't relationships be easy?" I finally asked.

He shrugged. "Would they be worth it if they were?"

"I just wonder how you ever know . . . this is the one." I told him about Amber's reading and the reason she'd bugged out on us.

"Sean liked her," he said.

"You want to hear the really weird thing?" I asked.

"There's something weirder than a psychic's

prediction and your friend freaking out because Tank has ink?"

"Well, maybe not weirder, but . . . well, the thing is, Amber has always talked about going to Rice. It's her first choice, and there's Sean . . . at Rice."

"Mmm. So maybe in another year or so . . ."

"Maybe."

"I'll let him know."

"No." I leaned back. "You can't do that. Then you're influencing it and making it happen."

"I've got something else I want to make happen."

And then he was kissing me again. I stopped thinking about Amber and Sean or Jenna and Tank. Or Sara and her predictions.

I was only thinking about how much I liked kissing Brady.

We left the restaurant at ten, which gave us an hour and a half before we had to meet up with Tank and Jenna and head back to the dorm. Neither of us was in the mood for the madness of Bourbon Street, so we just walked along the river. We could see the lights of the riverboats as they traveled along the Mississippi. It was all so romantic.

"You know, I don't even know your last name," I said, when we began walking back to the hotel.

"Miller."

I smiled at him. Brady Miller. I liked it.

"And yours?"

"Delaney," I responded.

"I thought you'd have an Italian-sounding name."

I grinned. "That's my mom's side of the family."

When we got to the lobby, Jenna and Tank were waiting for us. Tank drove us back to the dorm. While he walked Jenna to the door, Brady and I lagged behind.

"So being alone together wasn't so bad," I said.

He chuckled. "You really know how to stroke my ego."

I groaned. "I'm sorry. I just, I don't know, I just feel like I can say what's on my mind when I'm with you. That's a good thing, right?"

"Yeah, I guess."

"Seriously, though, I had a great time," I told him.

"Yeah, me, too."

Then he kissed me good night.

Chapter 15

Saturday we only worked until noon.

Tank drove us back to the dorm with the promise he and Brady would be back to get us in an hour. No way were we going to spend time in the French Quarter without getting cleaned up first. I was going through clothes like crazy. Tomorrow I definitely had to make time for laundry. Or else buy some more clothes.

Hmm. Buying more clothes might be the way to go.

I dressed in a denim miniskirt with cargo pockets on the sides so I could carry money and an ID without having to lug around my back-pack. I put on a tank with skinny straps, slipped on sandals, and used a banana clip to get my hair up off my shoulders. I picked one string of red beads to wear. I didn't think I'd be adding to my stash tonight, but I wasn't completely saying no to the possibility.

"Nice," Brady said to me when he and Tank picked us up.

We parked at their hotel, then started making our way through the French Quarter.

"I know just the place for lunch," Tank said. "The home of the original muffuletta."

Central Grocery had been housed in the French Quarter for nearly a century. As we walked inside the red emporium, the tantalizing aromas of salami, cheese, and garlic wafted around us. The worn floor creaked as we made our way around the aisles—displaying various containers of olives, pickles, and spices—to the counter where they took the food orders. The menu was pretty simple. Only one thing was served—the muffuletta. We ordered two to share, because the round sandwich is huge and piled with salami, ham, provolone, olive salad, and other special ingredients.

"Want to split a Barq's root beer?" Brady asked.

"Yeah. Thanks."

"Why don't you grab us some chairs?"

Off to the side was a counter with stools where people could eat. The store was small, the eating area even smaller, but we found four seats together.

"It smells really good in here," Jenna said.

"Yeah, it does."

"I am *so* hungry."

Brady took the stool beside me and unwrapped the sandwich. It was huge, cut into quarters. I had a feeling that one piece was going to be enough for me, and I wondered if we should have just ordered one for the four of us to share.

But Brady and Tank had monstrous appetites, and in no time the sandwiches were gone. They were delicious, and the root beer just topped it off.

I felt incredibly stuffed as we walked out of the store. I didn't think I could have eaten a pecan praline if it was given to me free. Okay, I could have. My theory is that sugar melts, so it doesn't fill you up.

Once we were outside, Jenna pulled me aside.

"Tank and I were thinking of going off and

doing our own thing, but I wanted to make sure you were okay with that, with being alone with Brady."

"That's cool."

"You sure?"

"We've been alone before," I reminded her.

"I know. I just didn't know if you wanted a lot of alone time, because I was thinking we wouldn't hook back up until later tonight."

"I'm fine, Jenna."

"Okay, then, we'll catch up with you at the ghost tour."

She took Tank's hand and led him away.

"What was that about?" Brady asked.

I shrugged. "Just Jenna being silly. They want to do their own thing."

"I'm not surprised. He's got it bad for her." He suddenly looked guilty. "Don't tell her I said that. I mean, it should come from him."

"But it would give me a chance to play psychic," I teased.

"Don't. Please."

I pretended to think it over for a bit. Then finally I said, "Okay."

"You were never going to tell her, were you?"

Smiling, I shook my head.

Holding hands, Brady and I walked to the French Market. It's a covered flea market, so we were at least out of the sun. There were so many vendors.

"This probably isn't the place to be if we're going on a ghost tour tonight," I said, thinking of hauling anything I bought around all day.

"If you find something you want, we can always take it back to my room," Brady said.

"Do you like shopping?"

"Not particularly, but I really like people-watching, and this is a great place for that."

"So you're okay if I stop and look at stuff?" The one time I'd taken Drew shopping with me, he'd moped around and totally spoiled the day. He said guys had a gene that prevented them from having patience at a mall. I didn't buy into it, though, because my dad always went shopping with my mom.

"Look all you want," Brady said. "I've got no appointments to keep."

"Except for the ghost tour," I reminded him.

"Well, yeah, but that's not for a while yet."

We strolled up and down the aisles. A lot

of the vendors were craftsmen, displaying various items they'd made. Some of the vendors had really inexpensive products—knockoffs, trinkets.

Like Brady had said, the most fun was just watching the people, seeing their excitement when they discovered a find, listening to them haggling over prices.

"Hey, I was wondering if you'd do me a favor," Brady said after a while.

I gave him what I hoped was a sultry smile. "Depends what it is."

"I want to find something to take back to my youngest sister. I was hoping you could help me figure out what would be a good thing to get her."

Did he think all girls liked the same things? I didn't have a clue what his sister might like.

"How about a box of pralines?"

He shook his head. "She'd yell at me for screwing up whatever diet she's on when I get home."

"She yells at you?"

"Oh yeah."

"And you want to buy her something?"

He shrugged. "It's what brothers do."

"Not mine."

"You have a brother?"

"Yeah, but he's twelve."

He grinned. "He's probably too young to appreciate you."

"Maybe." I squeezed his hand. "There's so much we still don't know about each other."

It was weird, because we hadn't grown up in the same town or gone to the same school. I didn't know all the details of his life, but I felt like I knew him.

"What's there to know? I have a mom and a dad and three sisters, one who likes to get presents. I go to Rice, majoring in architecture. And I like you. A lot."

He made it all seem so simple, and I knew that he probably wanted me to say back that I liked him . . . a lot. But I couldn't. Even if it was true. So instead I asked, "Why the Kansas City Chiefs?"

"What?"

"Your hat." He wasn't wearing it today. "Why that team?"

"My oldest sister lives in Kansas City now.

I went to visit her, went to a Chiefs game."

"So you're not necessarily a fan?"

"Nope, Houston Texans all the way. So, you and I have something in common."

"Uh, actually we don't. That first night at dinner, I just said that to have something to say. I'm not really into football."

"That's just un-Texan."

I knew what he meant—in Texas, football is king.

I grimaced. "Yeah, I know."

"Might have to do an intervention here. Take you to a Rice game."

It was the first time he'd said something— anything—that hinted at us seeing each other when our time here was finished.

My concern must have shown on my face, because he said, "Sorry. Forgot. We're just summer buddies, right?"

I nodded. "Yeah, just for the summer. That was our agreement."

He studied me for a minute. "Okay. Let's go souvenir shopping."

We stopped at a table of handcrafted jewelry.

He spent about twenty minutes looking over the various selections, asking me my opinion. My favorite piece was a delicate silver chain threaded through a fleur-de-lis charm.

He decided to buy it for his sister.

"I trust your judgment. If you like it, she will, too," he said.

"She might not."

"She will."

"Do I remind you of your sister?"

He scoffed. "No. No way."

"So our tastes might not be the same."

"I can tell you they're not. You have better taste."

He always made me feel good about myself.

"My pockets are a little roomier," I said. "Want me to carry it for you?"

"Sure. Thanks. Good thing I didn't get her a box of pralines, huh?"

I laughed. "Yeah."

We spent some more time walking by the stalls, looking at the various offerings. Then we slipped on our sunglasses and walked back into the sunshine.

It was hot and muggy so we went to the aquarium, to cool off in the air conditioning as much as to view all the exhibits. When we were walking, we'd hold hands. When we were simply standing, looking at something, Brady would slip his arm around me and hold me against his side.

Needless to say, I found an excuse to stand and watch a lot of things.

I loved the way that I fit up against him. My head nestled right into the little curve of his shoulder. His arm would come around me and he'd rest his hand on my stomach or my hip. And sometimes he'd kiss the curve of my neck and shoulder.

It all seemed so natural. So right. I couldn't imagine not being with him.

We rode the streetcar down to the Garden District, famous for its mansions. We got off the streetcar at one end and began walking back up toward the French Quarter. The nice thing about walking through the Garden District was that the area had so many trees we were almost always walking in the shade.

"I think that's Anne Rice's house," Brady said when we got to the corner of First Street and Chestnut.

It was a white two-story house with a balcony on the second floor.

"She lives in California now," I said.

"But doesn't this seem like the perfect place to write about vampires and witches?" Brady asked.

"Yeah, it does."

"Wonder if it'll be on the tour tonight."

I shrugged. "Have you ever been on a ghost tour?"

"Nope. How about you?"

"No. I'd say I was skeptical, except after Sara's reading, I have a feeling that after tonight, I'll believe in ghosts."

Brady chuckled. "Yeah, I know what you mean."

We were walking along, holding hands again.

"I didn't think you believed in psychics," I said.

"I don't . . . or at least I didn't. But yours seemed to be right on and the one I had—"

I stopped walking and pulled him back to face me. "You had a reading? You didn't say anything. When was this?"

"The day I met you."

"Was it with Saraphina?"

"No, someone else."

I grinned broadly. "Come on! Spill it! What did she tell you?"

He removed his sunglasses and held my gaze. He looked so serious that I got a little worried. What could she have told him? Was it bad news?

He cleared his throat, took a deep breath. "She said, 'For you, I see life is good.' Which didn't make any sense at the time, because some stuff was going on in my life that wasn't good, so I figured it was a con, something she probably said to everyone, but then . . ."

His voice trailed off, and I realized where this was going.

"My 'Life Is Good' hat," I whispered, goose bumps erupting along my arms, in spite of the heat of the afternoon.

He grinned. "Yeah."

"Spooky. Way spooky."

"Oh yeah."

I furrowed my brow. "What was bad in your life?"

He shook his head. "Nothing important, nothing that matters anymore, anyway. Now, life *is* good."

And he drew me close and kissed me. No doubt a ploy to stop me from prying into his past.

It worked, because when he kissed me, I could hardly think at all.

Chapter 16

We caught up with Tank and Jenna a little before nine in front of Sara—Saraphina's. It was hard to think of her with her psychic's name now that I knew her as a normal person. Almost normal, anyway.

As long as she didn't give me any secretive, off-the-record readings.

Amber was coming back, just as she'd predicted. But she'd also predicted some hurt when that happened. I didn't like the idea of that. Not at all. Although maybe it would be something simple, something not too painful — like another splinter, or a sunburn. Something small. But then, why bother to mention it?

Palling around with a psychic had its drawbacks. It was one thing for her to give me a reading when I was paying for it, but when she told me something she saw because she felt compelled to tell me—well, quite honestly, it made me worry.

Nearly a dozen people stood around, waiting for our hostess or tour guide or whatever she would be calling herself tonight.

"I don't believe in ghosts," Jenna said— three times—like a mantra.

Which made me think maybe she did believe in them. She sounded nervous. I knew she didn't like scary things.

"I have a feeling Sara will have us convinced before the night is over," Brady said.

"Yeah, well, just don't let go of my hand," I ordered. "And hold me close if I get scared."

"I hope you get scared," he said in a low voice near my ear.

"Me, too." A delicious shiver went through me. "I can practically guarantee it."

He was standing behind me, and he tightened his arms around my waist, pulling me closer. He dropped a kiss onto my bare shoulder.

Oh yeah, I might get scared, but it would be the good kind of scared, where we held each other close and laughed. Or maybe just kissed. I was starting to like him so much—and that scared me most of all.

When she finally arrived, Sara was dressed all in black, a black, hooded cloak swirling around her. It seemed like the fog was trailing in behind her. Her vibrant red hair was the only visible color. She was wearing it down and it flowed past her shoulders.

"Good evening," she said in a very melodramatic, haunting voice. "Does anyone not have a partner?"

Everyone was already paired up.

"Good," she said. "Now, I want you to hold your partner's hand and no matter what happens, don't let go. People have been known to disappear on the streets of New Orleans and never be seen again."

A chill went through me. Yeah, she was going to have us believing in ghosts.

"We are known as the most haunted city in the country," she continued. "And sometimes the spirits get jealous of the living. If you listen closely as we walk through the streets, sometimes you'll hear them crying, sometimes you'll hear them singing, sometimes you'll hear them dying."

I squeezed Brady's hand and rose up on my toes, so only he would hear me. "Are we sure we want to do this?"

"Oh yeah. And if you get so scared you need someone to sleep with you tonight — I'm there."

I didn't think I was going to get that scared, but who knew?

And okay, quite honestly, snuggling up with Brady appealed to me. It was frightening how quickly and how hard I was falling for the guy.

He was nice, he was fun, and he was hot. I just liked the way I felt when we were together. Like we were part of something.

"Follow me as we seek out the lost souls of New Orleans," Sara said in that spooky voice she'd perfected. It sent more chills over my flesh.

Must have sent chills over Brady's, too, because he put his arm around me, like holding hands wasn't enough to keep us from getting lost. We headed up Royal Street.

"New Orleans history is rich with haunt-ings. Some of the spirits are here because of something left undone. Some feel compelled to remain and re-create the circumstances of their death until justice has been gained. Most spirits are playful, causing mischief. Especially those who died as children. There are rare accounts of spirits causing harm, but rest assured that you'll all be safe tonight. The spirits know me, and they know we mean them no harm. That we mourn their passing, and that we're here to remember."

"That doesn't sound too bad," I whispered, starting to relax.

I felt something brush against my bare calf. I looked down, but there was nothing there. I shivered.

"You okay?" Brady asked.

"I thought I felt something."

"Like what?"

"A cat maybe. A very, very soft cat. It was just a light touch."

"Probably nothing."

"Probably."

But it hadn't felt like nothing.

"Over here we have a mansion that reflects our city's dark history," Sara said.

We stopped in front of a large gray building as Sara told us about Delphine Lalaurie and her physician husband. Wealthy, they were known for their lavish parties until it was discovered that they were monsters, performing surgical experiments on their slaves.

"Within the manor," Sara said, "there have been reported sightings of a man walking about carrying his head."

A shudder went through me.

"Is that what she calls being playful?" I whispered.

Brady chuckled. Did I sound spooked? I thought I sounded spooked.

"And on foggy nights, you can hear the screams of those who were abused within those walls. They are still crying out for justice."

Sara took us down Orleans Street, where on rainy nights the ghost of a priest who'd led a funeral procession to bury the remains of wrongly executed men could be heard singing.

Brady tightened his arms around me and rested his chin on my shoulder. I felt breath whisper across my neck. I told myself it was his. It had to be his.

"Thank goodness it's not raining," he said.

"Really."

"Are you believing this stuff?" He sounded totally stunned.

I twisted my head around. He was grinning.

"Don't you?" I asked.

"No. This is all bogus."

Was it? I didn't know anymore.

At 716 Dauphine Street, Sara told us about the ghost of a sultan who was murdered along with his wives and children and now haunted the four-story house.

"One of my favorite spirits remains here," she said. "I'm fairly certain it's one of the sultan's children. It likes to tickle necks."

I felt a light prickle over my neck. I hunched my shoulders and turned to Brady. "Don't."

"What?"

"I know you're trying to scare me."

"What are you talking about?"

What *was* I talking about? Because he was holding my hand, and no way he could have touched my neck without twisting around — and that I would have noticed.

Maybe it had been a moth or a mosquito. Some little insect of the night.

Every street she walked us along had tales of horrific murders—a man had killed his wife and the ghost of his wife had killed his mistress. What was that she'd said earlier about ghosts not causing harm?

Although the night was warm, I felt chilled. At one point, I thought I saw an apparition—a woman in a white nightgown—but it was gone so fast that I couldn't be sure.

When we'd circled back around to Sara's shop, she seemed really pleased with herself. Maybe because it looked like several people were pale. I probably was, too.

"In two weeks, John and I will take you on a vampire tour. He loves fresh blood! Sleep well," she said, before whipping her cloak around her and walking off. It seemed as if she disappeared from sight sooner than she should have.

"Okay, that was creepy," Jenna said.

"You mean the tour, or John liking fresh blood?" I asked.

"All of it. Sara was a little out there at the end."

"I can't see Ms. Wynder with a vampire," I said.

She laughed. "Me either."

I figured they'd laugh if I told them that I thought I'd felt something. So I kept quiet, but I couldn't stop thinking about it. New Orleans was definitely a city for those who believed in the supernatural. And even those who didn't could have their skepticism challenged.

"Anyone hungry?" Tank asked.

I wasn't, but I welcomed anything to take my mind off the tour.

We went to McDonald's. Not very New Orleans-ish, but it was late and they were open. And the lights were bright—I suddenly had a love of bright lights—so there were no spooky things lurking about.

And actually, once I bit into my burger, I realized that I was hungry. Very hungry. Apparently ghost hunting works up an appetite.

"I don't know if I'm going to do the vampire

tour," Jenna said as she swirled a fry in the ketchup. "I mean, I don't believe in vampires, but then I didn't believe in ghosts either, but that was before tonight. I think I saw one."

"Saw what?" Tank asked.

"A ghost."

He laughed so loudly that several other late-night customers looked over at our table.

"I saw something, too," I said, feeling a need to support Jenna. And okay. I *had* seen something.

"Probably just someone walking by," Tank said.

"If they want to believe in ghosts, I'm down with that," Brady said, scooting closer to me. "As a matter of fact, I'm not certain I want to sleep alone tonight."

"You're scared?" Tank asked.

Brady glared at him, and I laughed.

Then Tank widened his eyes. "Oh. Right. Right. Babe, if you're scared—"

"I might be," Jenna said, "but not if you're going to make fun of me."

They started talking low again, like Brady

and I weren't even there.

"Did you really see something?" Brady asked.

I shrugged, popped a fry into my mouth. "Maybe. I don't know. Could be the power of suggestion. I definitely felt something. On my calf, on the back of my neck."

"Me, too. On the back of my neck."

"Really?"

"No. But if it'll make you not want to sleep alone—"

I shoved playfully on his shoulder. "Get over it. That's so not happening."

We left McDonald's and started walking toward Bourbon Street, as though it was a given that that's where we wanted to end the night.

Since it was Saturday, Ms. Wynder had said she wouldn't do a bed check until two, and I wondered if she'd even bother. What if things got hot and steamy between her and John?

Tank and Jenna were behind us. Brady turned, walking backward. "Hey, we'll catch up with y'all later, at the hotel."

Then he quickened his pace, pulling me along with him. "Come on."

"Where are we going?"

"You'll see."

The guy was nothing but surprises, which I liked. Because every surprise was better than the one that came before.

He brought me around a corner, where a horse and carriage were waiting. The driver wore a top hat, very high society.

"Do you go down to the Garden District?" Brady asked him.

"Yes, sir."

"Hop in," Brady said to me.

Once he paid the driver, and we were settled against the leather seats with Brady's arm around me, I asked, "How did you know I wanted to do this?"

"It's a chick thing. All girls want to do it."

"Your sisters trained you right."

He laughed. "Yeah, but don't tell them that. I'll never hear the end of it."

And I wondered if I'd ever meet his sisters. It didn't seem likely. I mean, why would they come here? And in a few weeks, Brady and I would go our separate ways.

He wound his finger around my beaded

necklace. "So, are you planning to get more of these tonight?"

"I don't think so."

"Yeah. That's what I figured. So I didn't think Bourbon Street would be *that* much fun."

"Watching *you* get beads is fun."

"Yeah, but we should take turns."

That sounded like such a couple thing to say.

"I really had fun today," I said.

"Yeah, me, too."

I nestled my head against his shoulder.

"So tell me about your breakup," he said quietly.

I eased away from him a little and met his gaze. "What does it matter?"

He tucked my hair behind my ear. "I like you, Dawn. I think this guy, whoever he is, is still messing with you."

I looked at the driver. His back was to us. He wasn't paying any attention. And we were talking low. I sighed. "Drew. His name is Drew and he—" I shook my head.

"He what?"

It hurt to think about it, hurt even more to

say it. "He cheated on me."

"Okay."

"Okay? That's all? Aren't you going to tell me that he's a jerk?"

"You already know that."

Yeah, I knew that, but I still found some comfort in hearing it. And while I was usually okay with his single okay, right now I wanted more.

"What you need to understand," he said quietly, "is that I'm not him."

Then, with his hand cradling my cheek and his thumb stroking near the corner of my mouth, he leaned in and kissed me. Something about the kiss seemed different. Like all the others had been for fun, but this one was meant to be more.

It was kind of scary, but at the same time, I realized that it was something that I wanted.

I felt like I had on the ghost tour. Doubting what I was feeling. Wondering if it was real.

Or would it—like an apparition—disappear, and leave me wondering if it had truly ever been there?

Chapter 17

*I*t wasn't until Jenna and I were back in our dorm room—with thirty seconds to spare before the two o'clock curfew—and I was getting ready for bed that I remembered the necklace I'd put in my pocket for safekeeping.

I sat on the edge of the bed and looked at it again. It was really pretty. I wished I'd bought one for myself. Next week, I would. I was sure the vendor would still be there.

"What's that?" Jenna asked.

"Oh, a necklace Brady bought for his sister."

"He buys things for his sister? Wow. My brother doesn't know the first thing about buying me something."

"I helped him pick it out." Saying that

sounded weird. Like maybe we were shopping for something much more important.

"I'm really glad you're hanging out with him," Jenna said.

"Only because it means he's not hanging out with Tank all the time, and you have some time alone."

"Well, there is that. I'm so crazy about Tank, Dawn. It's scary sometimes."

"Tell me about it."

"But it's exciting, too. It's everything." She sat in the middle of her bed and brought her legs up beneath her. "Did you feel that way about Drew?"

Did I? Gosh, it was suddenly hard to remember. All I could remember now was being hurt and angry at him. Like that moment of seeing him with someone else had totally destroyed any good feelings I'd ever had for him. Had I been scared when he asked me out? Nervous? Excited?

"I can't remember, Jenna. That's so weird."

"You know, sometimes I think about what Sara said about you rebuilding. I thought she was talking about New Orleans. But what if she was talking about your heart?"

"She didn't know my heart needed rebuilding."

"She doesn't need to *know* stuff. She just sees things. She said you had to be careful with the tools. I thought she meant hammers and saws. What if she meant Brady?"

I flopped back on the bed. "You're really giving too much thought to all this."

"It's the puzzle solver in me. I can't help it."

I rolled my head to the side and looked at her. "She said I could get hurt. If I wasn't careful. Jenna, I don't think I've been careful. I think I've fallen for him."

"That's a good thing, Dawn. It means you're over Drew."

"No, it means I've set myself up to be hurt again. We agreed this was a Big Easy–only relationship."

"So, change the terms of your agreement."

"What if he doesn't want to?"

She sighed. "Do you have to doubt everything?"

I sat up. "Me? Doubting? You're the one trying to figure everything out, trying to solve the puzzles, wanting all the answers."

She came off the bed. "Well, I've never been in love before, and I don't know if I like it. I thought having a boyfriend would stop all the questions, but there's just more of them."

I smiled. "Yeah, it's a bummer, isn't it?"

"The future is just so"—she threw her hands up—"vague. There are just so many possibilities."

"And going to see a psychic sure doesn't help."

"No, it doesn't." She sat back down on the bed. "So what are we going to do?"

"You think *I* know?"

Laughing, she shook her head. "No, actually, I think you're probably more confused than I am."

"Well, thanks a lot."

Her cell phone rang and we both jumped. Then mine rang.

"Time for good-night calls," she said.

Okay, I guessed tonight we'd moved to a new level. I mean, we'd spoken that one night before I went to bed, but it had been on Jenna's phone, so it didn't really count. Oh, heck, maybe it did.

I answered, "Hey."

"Did I wake you?"

"No." I stretched out, rolled onto my side, and my knee touched the sack the necklace had been in. "I forgot to give you your sister's necklace."

"It's yours."

My brow furrowed. "What? No, I'm not talking about the beads, I'm talking about—"

"The fleur-de-lis."

"Yeah."

"I bought it for you. Why do you think I let you pick it out?"

"But you said it was for her."

"I thought you'd go all weird on me if I bought you something."

"Weird?" I said, offended. "I don't go weird."

"You go weird. You worry about what I really feel or what you really feel or what we're thinking. You're expecting me to hurt you, and I don't know how to make you stop expecting that."

I wrapped my hand around the charm. "I'm a mess. I don't know why you hang out with me."

"I hang out with you because I like you.

You're funny and fun and you believe in ghosts—"

"I don't believe in ghosts. I just had some weird stuff happen tonight."

"Are you sleeping with the light on?"

I hated to admit it, but—

"Yeah, we probably will. Jenna wants to." When in doubt, blame it on your friend. I figured we'd at least keep on the light in the bathroom with the door partially opened.

"About the necklace," I said.

"Yeah?" I heard the impatience in his voice, maybe even a little bit of anger. I couldn't imagine Brady being angry.

"Thank you. I really wanted one for myself, and this one will always be special. Remind me of my time here. My time with you."

"Good."

"But, you were very sneaky having me pick it out."

"I thought it was clever. If I'd known you longer, I might have known what to get, but we're on the short-term plan here. Right?"

"Yeah. Short term."

"End of summer."

"End of New Orleans." And that made me sad.

"Okay, then. See you tomorrow."

"What are we going to do?"

"I figure the least you can do is my laundry."

"What?"

He laughed. "No go, huh? I don't know what we'll do, but it'll be sometime in the afternoon. I do have to get my clothes washed. Maybe we'll just hang out by the pool."

"I like that idea. I could use a day of not doing anything."

"Okay. Then. Tomorrow."

"Yeah. Night."

I closed my phone, set it aside, sat up, and looked at the necklace. I could feel myself smiling. It was the smile of someone who was totally and completely happy. It was the smile of someone who wasn't worried about getting hurt.

I put the necklace on. It felt right. Suddenly everything did. I wasn't even worried about Saraphina's prediction.

But maybe I should have continued to worry about being careful.

Chapter 18

Things were coming along nicely on the house. We were getting to the details. Jenna and I were hammering the trim around the windows that had been replaced.

The four of us had spent last Sunday at a lake near where we were staying, just relaxing. Sometimes we got together after we were finished building for the day. Sometimes it was just Brady and me. It seemed like we could always find something to talk about. And when we weren't talking, we were kissing.

"Hey, catch!" Brady yelled.

I looked over, dropped the hammer, and caught the bottle of water he tossed my way. He'd set his watch to go off every hour and he brought me a bottle when he grabbed one for himself. I sat down on the edge of the porch, removed my safety goggles and hard hat, and set them aside. I twisted the cap and took a long swallow of the cold water. It tasted so good.

Brady leaned against the beam. I watched a droplet trail down his bare chest. A silly thing to be fascinated watching, but fascinated I was. Just about everything about him fascinated me.

"Do you have a sec?" he asked.

I felt my cheeks warm as I lifted my gaze to his, certain my brow was furrowed and a question was in my eyes. We'd been really good about not sneaking off for stolen kisses. I wasn't sure Jenna could say the same. From time to time, she disappeared. Tank was usually AWOL at the same time.

Brady jerked his head to the side. "I want to show you something."

"What?"

He grinned. "If I could tell you, I wouldn't have to show you. Come on."

I got up and walked beside him as he headed toward the street, then sauntered along the line of cars that was parked against the curb. He had a lazy stride — which was odd because I knew he wasn't at all lazy. He was probably one of the hardest workers here. Me, I took a break every fifteen minutes just to catch my breath, dip a towel into ice water, and wrap it around my neck to cool down. I couldn't imagine what it would be like around here come August. Next year, I thought, I'd do this volunteer work over spring break, when it wasn't quite as hot yet.

Yeah, I was already making plans to come back. I really liked New Orleans. It had so much to offer, and we hadn't even explored everything yet.

When we got to Tank's car, Brady stopped, reached into his back pocket, pulled something out, and held it toward me. It looked like white cardboard, folded in half.

"What is it?" I asked.

"Open it."

I set my water bottle on the trunk of the car, took the cardboard, and unfolded it. It was a colorful butterfly. A temporary tattoo. I laughed.

"I saw it at the convenience store where we stopped to get coffee this morning," Brady said. "It reminded me of you."

I squinted up at him. I hadn't put my sunglasses on. The sun was bright, but his smile was brighter.

"I see."

"I could put it on you if you want."

"What? Right now?"

His grin, if at all possible, grew wider. "Yeah. Why not? Lean on the trunk."

He took the towel from around my neck and poured some water from his water bottle on it. I glanced around. It seemed kind of wicked in a way, and sort of silly, too.

"Why not?" I repeated, handed him the tattoo, and leaned against the car. I lifted my T-shirt slightly and pushed the waistband of my jeans down just a tad, near my left hip.

I felt him lay the piece of paper against my skin, felt the damp towel against my back. "That's cold!"

"Bet it feels good, though," he said.

In no time at all he was peeling back the paper. "Perfect."

I moved around him and looked in the side-view mirror, twisting around slightly, so I could see my backside. All I could see was part of the wings peeking out above the waistband of my jeans.

"Sexy," Brady said.

His voice dropped a notch or two, and it sent a shiver along my spine. I'd never had a guy tell me I was sexy before. I liked it. I liked it a lot.

He put his hands on either side of my hips and drew me closer. "I had an ulterior motive in giving you the tattoo. Now I can say something innocent like, 'I'd like to see the bottom half of that tattoo.'" He wiggled his eyebrows. "And it might not be innocent at all."

"Yeah, well, you should have taken a good look at it when you were applying it, because that was probably the last time you'll see the bottom half." I stood on tiptoes and nipped his chin. He had a really nice chin. Strong, sturdy. It matched his strong jaw.

I'd always thought a guy's eyes were his best feature, revealed the most about him. But the truth was, there wasn't anything about Brady that I didn't think was darn near perfect.

"We'll see," he said in a low voice, like a challenge. I knew he was still talking about the tattoo and wanting to see all of it again.

Then he was kissing me, and I thought—
Yeah, we'll see.

A week later, I moved from hammering outside to painting bedroom walls.

I'd called Amber and given her the measurements for the windows and told her that I was going to paint the little girls' rooms pink. Brady had borrowed Tank's car to take me shopping for the paint. I'd bought it myself, because the builder who was donating the supplies had brought only cream-colored paint. And while cream is a nice neutral color, little girls should have something special.

I dipped the roller into the pan, then began rolling it over the walls again. When we'd first started working on the house it smelled of mildew and rot. Now it smelled of paint, of new. It smelled wonderful.

I'd never been involved in something that made me feel this good about myself.

"Hey, guess who just got here?" Jenna asked from the doorway.

I turned around, but before I could answer,

she said, "It's Amber. Come on."

I'd known that, of course. Just as Sara had predicted. Back from her doubts.

I was so ready to see her again. I hurried through the house—in Jenna's wake—and stepped out onto the porch. And there Amber was, running across the yard that when we'd first arrived had been littered. Now the house was almost completed.

I hopped off the porch and rushed to her, reaching her at the same time that Jenna did. We did a three-person hug, laughing. Hopping up and down. Going in a circle. I had so much to tell her. So much to share.

I wanted to hear about everything that had happened at home, too. She'd hardly called, so I knew she'd been wrapped up in Chad. That's the way it is when you have a boyfriend. You spend so much time with him. I wanted to hear it all.

She leaned back, and her smile dimmed. "I didn't come alone."

"I know. Saraphina told me you wouldn't," I said.

She frowned, worried, so typical. "She knew

I was coming back?"

I nodded. "With a guy with black hair."

I looked past her. At the black-haired guy standing a few feet away.

Drew.

The very last person I wanted to see.

I spun on my heel and walked back into the house, back to the bedroom I'd been painting.

Without saying a word to Drew. Without even acknowledging his existence, his presence, his intrusion on my life.

I picked up the roller and started rolling it over the wall in a frenzy—almost insanely. It was a little frightening really. But I thought the problem was that painting wasn't nearly as cathartic as hammering.

I really wanted to feel a hammer in my hand right now.

This place, this city, this house in a demolished neighborhood, had been my paradise. My sanctuary. It had been untainted. No memories of Drew. This was a Drew-less place.

I'd been happy. I'd been really happy.

I'd stopped thinking about Drew before I

went to sleep. I didn't want to see him, didn't want to talk to him, didn't want him to creep back into my life.

I heard footsteps. If it was Drew, I was going to pick up the can of paint and throw its contents on him.

"Dawn?"

It was Amber. I set down the roller, faced her, and crossed my arms over my chest. Jenna was standing beside her. Was she there to support Amber or me? I'd lost my boyfriend. Was I going to lose my friends?

"What were you thinking?" I asked. It was all I could do not to shout.

And knowing Amber, she probably hadn't been thinking.

"Chad and I broke up," she said.

"You're kidding?" Jenna looked dumbstruck.

"Why would she kid about that?" I asked. "And how does that even remotely begin to explain bringing Drew here?"

Ignoring me, Jenna asked, "Why did you and Chad break up?"

"Because I wanted to do something meaningful with my summer, and he wanted to rent DVDs for TV shows he hadn't seen and do season marathons. All the different seasons of *24*. All the different seasons of *Monk* and *Lost* and *Scrubs*. I just wanted more."

"But you told me that he was interested in coming," I reminded her.

"He said he was, but he really wasn't. He was just humoring me. He didn't really care about what I wanted."

"So you broke up with him?" Jenna asked.

Amber nodded. "Plus, I couldn't stop thinking about Sean."

"He's with Sara," I said.

I knew it was mean, but I took some satisfaction in telling her that. I was upset that she'd brought Drew here.

I know sometimes she says things that are out there, but this was beyond out there. This was plain stupid.

"Well, Sean's not *with* her, with her," Amber said. "I mean, I know they've been hanging out together, but they're just friends. She's way older than he is. And he's called me."

I couldn't believe this. Everything was such a mess.

"You broke up with Chad so you could get together with Sean?" Jenna asked.

Jenna still wanted details. I wanted Drew out of there.

"I broke up with Chad because watching TV isn't enough for me. And if Sean isn't the one Sara was referring to—what I'll have better in college—I'm okay with that. I just knew Chad was wrong."

"But you loved him."

Amber nodded. "I know it seems all screwed up, but I know I did the right thing."

"Maybe you did the right thing about Chad," I said, "but Drew? Why bring him?"

"Because I needed a way to get here, and he has a car," Amber explained.

"You could have flown, your parents could have brought you, you could have hitchhiked." Although I knew that was a dangerous option and really didn't want her to risk it—I was upset. Anything was better than seeing Drew again.

"He wanted to help out, though, so it seemed like a perfect solution."

I couldn't believe this. "Amber—"

"I know you're still mad at him, but you should at least talk to him. He's sorry—"

"Oh, he's sorry, all right."

"Prom night was a moment of weakness."

What a crappy excuse. I wasn't buying it. And while she wasn't usually good at figuring things out, she read the expression on my face perfectly.

"Look, he wants to get back together with you," she said.

"Ain't happening."

"But you need closure."

"I hate that word. I had closure. I slammed his car door *closed* and walked away."

"And never talked to him again?"

"There was nothing to say. There still isn't."

"I think you're wrong. I think there's a lot more to say."

No, there wasn't. There was nothing. Absolutely nothing. I didn't care about Drew anymore. I didn't care about him at all.

I headed for the door.

"Where are you going?" Amber asked.

"To take care of something."

I walked into the kitchen where Brady and some other guys were supposed to be working.

And there was Drew.

The guys were standing around talking to him, but I knew that nothing he said was important. Everything was a lie. Especially when he said he loved you.

Brady stepped out of the circle just a little bit when he saw me.

Drew turned around and took a step toward me, his hands out, his smile . . . God, it looked so fake, so stupid. How had I ever trusted it?

"Dawn—"

I walked right by him. Totally ignoring him. I went up to Brady, wrapped my arms around his neck, and kissed him.

Energetically, thoroughly. Maybe even a little desperately.

He pulled back and gave me a funny look. Then he took my hand. "Come on."

He led me past Drew, whose mouth was hanging open.

Good, I thought. *Now you know how it feels.*

♥ ♥ ♥

"What was going on back there?"

Brady was leaning against Tank's car, his sunglasses on, his arms crossed over his chest.

"I was missing you."

"Dawn, I deserve better than that."

I looked down at the grass and could see some shards of broken glass. Would we ever get everything cleaned up?

"He was your boyfriend, wasn't he?"

Nodding, I looked up.

"You were trying to make him jealous."

Well, okay, maybe I was. Maybe I wanted him to see what he gave up.

"Which means you still feel something for him," Brady finished.

"I don't! Not at all. He's such a jerk!" I felt tears burn my eyes. "I hate him."

"Hate's a feeling."

"It's not a good feeling. It's not like I care."

"Why's he here?" Brady asked.

"He gave Amber a lift. He wants to help."

"That's it?"

His voice dripped with skepticism. This was a side of Brady I'd never seen. Impatient.

I shifted from one foot to the other, while I decided whether to confirm what he suspected. "He wants us to get back together."

"Do you?"

I stared at him. "No. No way."

"Are you sure?"

"Yes."

"I'm not."

"You're not what?"

"Not so sure you don't want to get back together with him."

"Are you saying I'm a liar?"

"I think you were using me back there. Maybe I've been using you, too, but you need to figure out how you really feel about him."

Using me? How had he been using me?

"Because if you want to make him jealous," he continued, "it's because you want him back. I've been there, done that, and I'm not doing it again."

"I don't know what you're talking about. What are you saying?"

"I'm saying that we're over."

Chapter 19

*B*rady walked over to Tank, talked to him, then they came back, got in the car, and drove away.

Just like that.

It was just as I suspected: All guys eventually turned into jerks.

It was the opposite of the frog turning into the prince. Eventually, no matter what you did, the prince turned back into a frog.

"Dawn?"

Drew. Behind me.

Even his voice grated on my nerves. Without even looking at him, I started walking toward the house.

"I'm really, really sorry," he said.

I kept walking.

"Won't you even talk to me?" he asked.

Nope.

I just kept walking.

I saw Amber leaning against the new wall of the house, talking to Sean. Smiling. Laughing. He was tucking her hair behind her ear.

At least she'd broken up with Chad, before getting more involved with Sean. I was sure it had been hard to break up with him, and he was probably hurt. But it was easier to get over a breakup than a betrayal.

Or at least I hoped it was.

Right now I was still reeling from Brady's outburst.

What was up with that anyway?

He'd broken our bargain.

Creep.

I felt tears sting my eyes. He wasn't a jerk or a creep. Not by a long shot.

But where had the guy who'd always been "okay" with everything gone?

Jenna came out of the house, hopped off the porch, and came over, stopping me from going wherever it was I was going.

I had no idea.

I was in shock.

"Are you okay?" Jenna asked.

"Brady left. He just left."

"Yeah, I know. Tank called to let me know."

"I don't get it. He's been so understanding—this whole time. And now, when I really need him, he just goes ballistic."

It was a little scary to realize how much I'd come to depend on him being there. That was so not what I'd planned for the summer.

Amber had left Sean and joined us.

"I'm sorry," she said. "I thought you'd be happy to see Drew."

"How could you possibly think that?" I asked.

"I just thought since he wanted to be with you again—"

"But I told you I was with Brady."

"Yeah, but I thought it was just for the summer."

It was. It was. But still.

It was hard to stay mad at Amber. She just didn't think, and I knew she hadn't meant to mess things up for me. But still, she had.

"Brady didn't even give me a chance to

explain," I said. "He just said it was over."

Jenna sighed. "Probably because of Melanie. Don't you think?"

My heart did a little stutter. "Melanie? Who's Melanie?"

Jenna looked surprised. Startled, even. "He didn't tell you about Melanie?"

Shivers went all through me. This was worse than thinking I felt a spirit tickle me on a ghost tour.

"Nooo. What's this about?"

She grimaced. "Oh, I don't know if I should tell you, then."

"Jenna! I need to understand what's going on here."

"Let me call Tank and see if it's okay for me to tell you."

"You need Tank's approval to help your friend?"

"He told me, but I don't know if I can tell you."

"Jenna."

She sighed. "Oh, all right. Melanie was Brady's girlfriend."

"He had a girlfriend?"

She nodded.

Why was I surprised he'd had a girlfriend? Honestly I would have been surprised if he hadn't. I mean, he had way too many smooth moves never to have had one. And he was so cute and nice. Of course he'd had a girlfriend.

"When?" I asked.

"I don't know all the details. Tank just told me about how she broke up with Brady—because it was such a cold way to do it."

"What'd she do?"

"She text-messaged him. He's in class and he gets a text message: 'I'm back with Mike.'"

"Back with?" I repeated.

"Yeah, apparently, she broke up with her boyfriend, then she was dating Brady, then she got back with the other guy."

"Did Brady like her? I mean, a lot?"

She nodded. "Think so."

"This is so weird," Amber whispered. "I don't know if I should have come back."

"You should have come back," I reassured her. "You just shouldn't have brought Drew."

"No, don't you get it? Saraphina said there

would be things hidden. I thought she meant that stupid snake," Amber said.

Another shiver went through me.

Secrets were things hidden. And Brady had one.

Why hadn't he told me?

Then I remembered him saying how he hadn't believed the psychic because life wasn't good. But he hadn't explained why.

I'd finally discovered his flaw.

My old boyfriend showed up and Brady just assumed I'd get back together with Drew.

He was as untrusting of girls as I was of guys.

Weren't we a terrific pair?

I'd never questioned why he'd been so agreeable to the terms of our agreement. Why a New-Orleans-only-no-breakup-predetermined-good-bye had been okay with him. Now I knew.

He was as scared of getting hurt again as I was.

"So what are you going to do?" Jenna asked.

"I don't know. I just . . . I just need to take some time." I looked at Amber. "Go talk to

Sean. That's the reason you came back. And Jenna, go finish painting the bedroom. I'm just going to . . . I don't know."

I walked away, walked across the yard to where we kept the ice chests. I opened one, searched through the icy water until I found a bottle. I closed the chest, twisted off the cap, took a long swallow.

It didn't help. My knees still felt weak. I sat on the chest.

Maybe I'd just go home. Who needed this aggravation?

Drew being here when I didn't want him to be. Brady believing that I'd get back together with Drew—just because he'd shown up.

Only I didn't want to go home. I wanted to be here. I wanted to build a house. I wanted to be with my friends. I wanted to explore the city more.

I'd run away once before because it had hurt too much to stay. But now, no matter how much it hurt to be here, I wasn't willing to leave.

I was vaguely aware of someone opening one of the other ice chests, the pop of a top being twisted off a bottle, the moan of the chest as someone sat on it.

"Sometimes I hate it when the things I see really do happen."

I looked over to find Sara sitting next to me.

"Amber's back," she said quietly. "And the black-haired guy with her? He broke something, didn't he?"

Oh yeah, big time.

Sara looked sad. As sad as I felt.

I nodded. "He used to be my boyfriend. And Brady was just so un-Brady about it. Do you happen to know any voodoo?"

A corner of her mouth quirked up. "Voodoo?"

"Yeah. I was thinking maybe a spell that would send Drew away and bring Brady back."

"You take three hairs from each of their heads, bury them in a backyard"—she jerked her thumb over her shoulder—"like this backyard, and jump up and down on the spot three times."

I looked at her, my eyes wide. "Really?"

She smiled. "No. It's never that simple, Dawn."

"Brady probably wouldn't give me three

strands of his hair anyway. He's kind of protective of his hair. He has this fear of going bald."

She shook her head. "Huh. I don't see him without hair."

I straightened up. "You mean, he's not going to go bald?"

She laughed. "Oh no, I don't *see* him, see him. I just can't imagine him bald."

"Oh. I thought if I gave him some good news . . ."

What did it matter? It didn't.

I sighed. "I don't suppose you see how all this is going to end."

She slowly shook her head. "Sorry."

I nodded. "That's okay. Sometimes it's probably better not to know."

"Yeah, sometimes it is."

And the way she said it made me think she knew more than she was letting on.

"I hate leaving you alone," Jenna said.

We were back in the dorm. I was sitting on the bed.

"I'll be fine."

Amber shifted her weight from one foot to the other. "You sure?"

Tank and Sean were coming to get them for a night of listening to bands. I wondered what Brady was going to be doing. I was a little afraid to ask.

So I didn't ask.

So typical of me. Not wanting to face the truth.

I could see him dancing shirtless on Bourbon Street, gathering beads. I wondered whose neck he'd put them around.

I wondered why he didn't tell me about Melanie.

It was strange, so strange, that all I could think about was him. How much I wanted to be with him.

After Jenna and Amber left, I just looked at the ceiling and thought about him.

When my phone rang, my heart gave a little jump—until I saw who was calling.

Drew.

I almost didn't answer. Mostly because, suddenly, nothing was there. The anger that I'd felt earlier—it was just gone.

"Hey."

"I didn't think you'd answer," he said.

"Then why did you call?"

"Just in case you did. I really want to see you, Dawn."

"Okay."

"Okay? You mean it?"

"Yeah." I gave him the address for the dorm. I changed into jeans and a knit top.

I was waiting outside the dorm when he drove up.

It was kind of funny. There was no excitement. No anticipation. It wasn't at all like waiting for Brady.

I walked over to his car and got in.

"Where do you want to go?" Drew asked.

"McDonald's."

"Seriously?"

"Yep."

I told him there was one near the French Quarter. As he drove, neither of us talked. There seemed to be so much to say and nothing to say.

I showed him where to park.

"Seems like we ought to eat someplace, I don't know, Cajun, I guess," he said as we crossed the street.

"I like this place because the lights are bright. I want to see you."

That seemed to please him. Maybe it sounded like a romantic thing to say, but romance had nothing to do with it. I just wanted to be able to see him clearly when we talked. Wanted him to see me, so there'd be no misunderstanding about what was being said.

Sometimes in the dark, you can misunderstand things.

He ordered a burger and fries. I ordered a soft drink.

"That John guy, he's nice. He found me a place to stay, with some other volunteers," Drew said once we were sitting in a booth.

"Amber said you came here because you wanted to help."

"Yeah. That, and to see you."

I really, really, really wanted nothing more than for him to go back to Katy. But at the same time, I couldn't help but think of him as an extra pair of hands. And New Orleans needed all the helping hands it could get.

So I wasn't here to tell him to leave. I was here to figure out how I could work with him. I didn't think it was going to be as hard as I'd envisioned.

"I thought you wanted to spend the summer doing water parks," I said.

"Yeah, me, too. But I was reading Jenna's blog—"

"Thanks for sending my mom that picture, by the way."

He blushed. "This afternoon, it looked like you were still seeing the guy."

"Yeah, I am." Or I would be, once I figured that part of my life out. I wasn't going to give Brady up nearly as easily as I'd given up Drew. I wasn't going to walk away without talking to him.

"How serious?" Drew asked.

"Serious enough." My arrangement with Brady wasn't any of Drew's business. "I just want you to know that I'm fine with you being here. I'm fine with you helping. I just need you to understand that you and I are over."

I thought about asking what had been wrong with me because I'd always thought it was somehow my fault. But now I knew there was nothing wrong with *me*. There had just been something wrong with *us*.

There wasn't much else to say after that. He drove me back to the dorm.

It may seem cold, but I didn't even bother with good-bye. I just got out.

I heard his door open.

"Dawn?"

I looked back over my shoulder. He just stood there.

"I'm really sorry. About prom night. You have to believe that. I was just getting so much attention from girls after being in the play that I let it go to my head. You were the one."

"Actually, Drew, I wasn't. If I was, you probably wouldn't have kept looking at the menu."

"What?"

I smiled, shook my head. "Just something Jenna said once."

"Are you sure you don't want to give it another shot?"

"You broke my heart, Drew."

"Dawn —"

"You. Broke. My. Heart. We're over. Completely and absolutely."

Now all I had to do was figure out what I was going to do about Brady.

I was lying on the AeroBed reading when Jenna and Amber came back to the room, just before midnight.

"You can have the bed," Amber said.

"Nah. Our original arrangement was that you got the bed, I got the air mattress."

"You don't sound mad at me anymore."

I sat up straighter, folded my legs beneath me. "I'm not. I saw Drew tonight."

They both sat on the floor.

"What happened?" Jenna asked.

I told them about our trip to McDonald's.

"You're not going to get back with him?" Amber asked.

I didn't know how many different ways to say it, so I just said, "No."

She looked confused.

"Are you going to get back together with Chad?" I asked.

"Absolutely not."

"There you are."

"But I left Chad on my terms."

"And tonight I left Drew on mine." Maybe in her spacey sort of way, she'd been right. I had needed some closure where Drew was concerned.

"So you're back with Sean?" I asked.

She nodded. "Yeah. I can't believe how much I missed him. And how much I missed you guys. I even missed the work. I'm thinking about going into construction after I graduate."

"Seriously?"

She nodded.

"But you left before we got to the really hard stuff."

"I know. But just the idea of it, of building. It's something I really want to do. Besides, there are women builders."

"I think that's great," Jenna said. "I'm glad you're back."

"Me, too," Amber replied. She peered at me.

"I am, too." I smiled at her. I knew what it was to worry about what someone thought about you.

"So what are you going to do about Brady now?" Jenna asked.

"Do some rebuilding."

Chapter 20

Much to my surprise, Drew was at the site the next morning. I hadn't really expected him to stay. He was wearing shorts, a T-shirt, and flip-flops. Like maybe he was on his way to a water park. So maybe he wasn't staying.

He walked up to me.

"Hey," he said.

"Hey."

In a way, it was sad that I felt so little for him.

"So what do I do?" he asked.

"What?" Did he still have hopes of us getting back together? Had I not been abundantly clear last night?

He flapped his hand around. "Around here. How do I help?"

"Uh, well, you should probably go talk to

263

John." *And John is going to tell you to go home and change into jeans and boots*, I thought. Drew really seemed clueless about what was involved in working here.

"Can't I just help you?"

"It doesn't work that way." Usually. Well, okay, if Brady had wanted to help me, I would have welcomed him. "John gives the assignments."

And I'd totally kill him if he assigned Drew to me.

"Okay. I'll see you around, then."

"Yeah."

It was only after Drew walked away that I saw Brady standing a short distance away, watching us.

He turned and went into the house, and I wondered what he thought he'd witnessed.

I went to the bedroom to finish painting. Amber had brought curtains and rods. As soon as we were done with the walls, we were going to hang everything up.

We still had a way to go with the last wall when I decided to take a water break. I went out the front door to the ice chests and grabbed four bottles of water. I walked back into the house, went into the kitchen, and waited while Brady and a couple of other guys finished putting up a cabinet. As soon as he turned around, I said, "Brady, catch."

I tossed him a bottle of water. He caught it, no problem. He had good reflexes—which I already knew.

He studied me, like he was trying to figure out what I was doing.

I just walked out and went back to painting the bedroom.

An hour later, I did the same thing—taking him a bottle of water like he'd always brought one to me.

When we finished painting the bedroom, I went back to the kitchen.

"You guys finished with the ladder?" I asked.

"Sure," one of them said.

I closed it up, tried to carry it—and discovered it was a lot more awkward than it looked.

I heard Brady sigh. Not sure how I recognized his sigh, but I did.

"I'll get it," he said, lifting it. "The legs, remember, it's all in the legs."

He carried it to the bedroom. "Where do you want it?"

"By the window."

Jenna and Amber were in the room, reading the directions for how to hang the curtain rod.

I took one of the brackets, some nails, and a hammer. I climbed up the ladder.

"Do you even know what you're doing?" Brady asked.

Not really, but still I said, "Oh yeah."

How hard could it be to put up a bracket?

I put the bracket against the wall, put the nail in the little hole, brought the hammer back—

"You've got—" Brady began.

And I missed the nail, slamming the hammer against my thumb.

"Ow!"

I jerked back, lost my balance, released a little shriek, fell—

And suddenly found myself in Brady's arms.

"Are you okay?" he asked.

I couldn't help it. Tears started burning my eyes and I shook my head. My reaction had nothing at all to do with the pain in my thumb. It had everything to do with the pain in my heart.

He set my feet on the floor and took my hand. "How bad is it?"

Out of the corner of my eye, I saw Amber and Jenna sneak out of the room, like partners in crime worried about getting caught. If I'd thought it was possible, I'd have thought they arranged all this. But it wasn't possible.

"Doesn't look too bad," Brady said.

I hadn't planned on hitting my thumb. I hadn't planned on ending up in Brady's arms.

"Looks can be deceiving," I said. "I know you saw me talking to Drew."

"You don't have to explain. His being here says it all." He moved away, picked up the hammer that I'd dropped.

"Actually it doesn't say anything," I said. "He's staying to work on the house. Not because of me."

"Yeah, right." He picked up the nail and

bracket. He climbed the ladder and began hammering the bracket into place.

"Are you pretending that's my head?"

He looked down at me. "What?"

"I used to pretend every nail was Drew."

"So you spent the summer thinking about him."

That confession had backfired.

"Only at first. And yes, yesterday, I was mad when I saw him. It was just the shock of it. And yes, I kissed you to try to hurt him. But he doesn't mean anything to me. Not anymore."

"I can't do this." He climbed down the ladder and handed me the hammer. "I just can't do it."

My heart almost stopped. For a minute, I thought he was leaving. Permanently. Going back to Houston.

But I found him in the kitchen, working on the cabinets. Not that he saw me.

I just peered in the open doorway, saw him, and thought, *Okay.*

Then I went to find Sara.

Saturday, Jenna and Amber spent the day shopping with me and walking around the French Quarter.

I told them that they didn't have to. I was okay with them spending the day with their guys. But they didn't want me hanging around the city by myself.

Besides, the three of us hadn't had much time together since that first day.

At least that was their reason. But I knew the truth. They were worried about me.

The past couple of days at the site had been a strain. To say the least. Mostly because I wasn't giving up on Brady.

I took him water every hour. Sometimes I'd just toss the bottle to him. Sometimes I'd stop and talk with him for a minute. Not about anything important. Not about us. Not about Drew.

He'd hold up the water bottle. "You don't have to do this."

"I know. I want to, though." And I'd decided that wanting to do something was enough reason to do it.

And tonight I was going on the vampire tour.

Because I wanted to.

I wanted to because Brady was going on it, too.

Sara had confirmed that for me earlier in the week—after the falling off the ladder incident. I hadn't asked her for a reading. I hadn't wanted her to confirm my future. Or not confirm it. Or give any hints. All I wanted her to do was pair me up with Brady.

And I'd take care of the rest.

Tank and Sean were going to be there as well. Jenna and Amber were going to meet up with them then. And hopefully, if my plan worked out . . . well, I just hoped it would.

So after a day of shopping and talking, we headed to Sara's.

I hadn't expected Drew to be there. I really needed to put a hex on the guy.

He smiled brightly when he saw us. "Hey!"

I just wiggled my fingers.

"This is going to be fun," he said.

"Yeah, it is."

Sara came over—dressed in her black cape

again—and took his arm. "You're going to be with me."

"Really?" he asked.

She winked at me. "Really."

She led him away.

"That was close," Jenna whispered.

Too close. I figured if Brady had seen Drew talking to me—he probably would have walked on by. But the guys weren't there yet.

"They are coming, aren't they?" I asked.

"Absolutely," Jenna said, looking at her phone. "Tank just texted. They're on their way."

I took a deep breath and adjusted the tote bag on my shoulder. "Okay."

Then I saw them crossing the street. They were heading right for us. Brady wasn't trying to avoid me, probably because Tank and Sean were leading the way and he was just following, not really looking the group over. I was standing a little behind Jenna and Amber, so he didn't see me until it was too late.

"Hey," I said.

"Hey."

Sara walked through the group, matching

people up. "Brady, you and Dawn."

She didn't even give him a chance to object.

"Your boyfriend's up there if you want to switch partners," Brady said.

"He's not my boyfriend. He *was*. Past tense. No more."

"You really think you mean that, don't you?"

"I don't *think*. I know." Had I been this obstinate in the beginning about wanting to have a dateless summer? Yeah, I guess I had been.

"Okay, everyone, shh . . . ," Sara said.

John suddenly appeared. It was like one minute he wasn't with us, the next he was.

I don't know how he did that, but I jumped. Brady snickered.

"Are you going to hold my hand if I get scared?" I asked.

He looked at me. He wasn't holding my hand now. I really, really missed him holding my hand.

"I believe in vampires," I said. I'd believe in just about anything if he'd hold my hand again.

"All right, people," John said. He was dressed in a flowing cape. And yes, he had fangs. And he looked pale—bloodless even. "Tonight, I'm going to give you an experience you'll never forget. Follow me."

He started walking down the street, and everyone fell into step behind him.

Everyone except Brady and me.

"Do you really want to do the tour?" I asked.

"Not really. You?"

I shook my head. "I'd rather go sit by the river." I lifted my tote. "I brought a blanket."

"Okay."

We turned and headed toward the Mississippi. He took my hand.

It was a start.

It was late, and night, and dark, and sultry. Even the breeze coming across the water was warm. Sometimes we could hear people laughing or music coming from the decks of the lighted riverboats.

Brady and I were sitting on the blanket.

273

We'd stopped at one of the many tourist haunts and bought a bottle of water. Just one. For the two of us.

Another step in the right direction.

We'd been sitting there for a while, though, neither of us saying anything. It wasn't uncomfortable. Or at least, I didn't feel that way.

I brought my knees up and wrapped my arms around my legs. "I went to a voodoo shop today."

"A voodoo shop."

I heard the skepticism in his voice. I turned my head, lay my cheek on my knees. "Yeah. Want to see what I got?"

"You bought something?"

"Uh-huh." I reached into my bag and brought out a candle. "If you light this, it keeps the bad mojo away." I set it down near my feet.

Then I brought out another candle. "And this one brings in the good mojo."

"Do you even know what mojo is?" he asked.

"Not really. I think it's like karma. Do you want to light them and see what happens?"

"Sure."

I struck a match, lit one, and then the other.

Brady lifted the first one, studied it. "This smells like peach."

With the flame flickering so close, I could see his face more clearly now.

"Is this really a voodoo candle?" he asked.

I shook my head. "No. But I've learned that sometimes what you believe is more important than what is real. I mean, if I believed that ghosts were really touching me, it didn't matter if it was a moth. And if you believed that I'd get back with Drew, it didn't matter that I wouldn't. You believed it. But you have to understand. I'm not Melanie."

He blew out the flame. "Who told you about Melanie?"

"Tank told Jenna. She told me. Why didn't *you* tell me?"

"What was there to say?"

"I don't know. But you were asking about Drew. So it seems like you should have said something about her."

He sighed. "She doesn't matter."

"Neither does Drew."

And maybe he'd been agreeable to my only-while-we're-here terms because they made him feel as safe as they made me feel. No commitment. No breakup. No heartache.

"We had an agreement," I said quietly. "I'm still in New Orleans. So unless you're planning to leave—"

"I'm not leaving."

"Okay then. I've got you for three more weeks."

"And what's-his-name?"

"I'm not interested in him at all."

He shook his head. "I don't usually overreact to things. But all I could think was that the boyfriend was here and you'd hook back up. I guess I wanted to get out first, on my own terms."

Which I understood completely.

"But our terms are . . . as long as we're in New Orleans," I reminded him.

"And we're still in the Big Easy," he said.

I nodded.

"Okay then."

He leaned in, touched my cheek. "I'm sorry if I was a jerk."

I smiled. "Even Dr. Phil has a bad day now and then. Besides, the reason I was kissing you in the kitchen was wrong. You were right about that."

"I've really missed you," he said.

He leaned in closer and kissed me.

I couldn't have been happier. Not only were we back on speaking terms, we were back on kissing terms.

Chapter 21

I couldn't believe that we'd completed our first house.

The hammers were silent, the rubbish carted away. We'd planted two spindly trees.

The house itself was painted. Inside, it was sparsely furnished. But it did have curtains hanging from the windows to give it a welcoming touch. I had bought some dolls and put them in each of the pink bedrooms.

All the many volunteers stood on the lawn, near the front porch, waiting for the residents to return.

Brady was holding my hand, but then he usually did. He knew that I wasn't going to leave him for Drew. And not only because

Drew was no longer there.

Drew had decided to go back home after only a week in the Big Easy. At least he'd helped for a while.

I couldn't say I particularly liked him, but I did know that I didn't hate him anymore.

The funny thing was—after that first day, having Drew around really didn't bother me. He was not a part of my life any longer.

Brady was.

Things between us were . . . well, developing. We spent most evenings together, going somewhere to listen to a band or a musician.

I was noticing everything about him. I knew he put his sunglasses on two seconds before he stepped into the sun. Always.

I noticed that he looked great in wrinkled T-shirts. And all his T-shirts were wrinkled. Even right after he washed them, because his sorting system was one pile for clean clothes, one pile for dirty clothes.

"Folding, hanging stuff up—not how I want to spend my time," he'd told me.

Yeah, I'd been in his room a couple of times.

To watch pay-on-demand movies. And cuddle without everyone in New Orleans looking on. He never pushed, but he hinted that he was interested in seeing the bottom half of my tattoo—even though it was long gone.

I was thinking about getting another one. A permanent one. One that would be there when I was ready to share it with him.

Now, Jenna and Tank were standing near us. So were Amber and Sean. It was kind of funny that so many couples were around, that so many of us had bonded while building.

A car pulled up in front of the house, and a thrill shot through me. I couldn't believe how excited I was that the family was coming home. That we'd done what we could to ensure that they were able to come home.

John went to greet them. Holding her daughters' hands, the woman walked to the house and stepped up on the porch. She was younger than I'd expected her to be and pretty. She turned to face us, with tears in her eyes.

"Thank you," she said. "Thank you . . . so much."

We clapped and cheered, acknowledging her—that she was home again. That we were all glad.

John opened the door for her, and she walked inside. I could hear the patter of her daughters' feet as they raced through the house.

"Mama! My room is pink!" one of the girls shouted. "I love pink!"

Brady put his arm around me, hugged me. "Good choice," he said.

My throat was tight. All I could do was nod, as tears filled my eyes. I felt a little guilty that I'd originally planned to spend my summer going to water parks. If Drew hadn't been such a jerk, that's what I would have done. And I would have missed out on this sense of accomplishment.

John stepped out on the porch and clapped his hands. "All right, people! Your job is done. Enjoy the rest of the day. We start on the next one in the morning!"

Tank, Jenna, Brady, and I walked to Tank's car. Sean and Amber were catching a ride with Sara. We seldom rode with Ms. Wynder anymore. But, then, she was usually with John.

As we were driving away, I looked out the back window and watched the mother and her daughters waving at us from the front porch. Her daughters were clutching the dolls I'd left in their rooms. I felt . . . happy.

Wiping the tears from my eyes, I leaned my head back on the seat. "One down, and about a thousand to go."

"I think there's more than a thousand," Brady said.

I rolled my head to the side and looked at him. "How many houses do you think there are that need to be rebuilt?"

He shrugged. "A lot."

"Even after all this time?"

"Oh yeah. It takes a long time."

Yeah, I thought, looking at him, rebuilding does take a long time. But it was worth it. It was so worth it.

"I am so glad we decided to spend part of our summer here," Amber said, later that night, as we were holding our own celebration.

She, Jenna, and I were sitting on a park

bench. A jazz band was playing nearby. The guys had decided to take a walk around, do some people-watching.

I think they knew that we wanted some time alone.

"Yeah, me, too," I said, fingering the fleur-de-lis on the necklace that Brady had given me. I wore it all the time.

"This has been the best summer ever," Jenna said.

"And it's not over," I pointed out. "We've still got another week to go."

"Now that we know what we're doing, maybe the next house will go faster."

"Maybe."

"You want to hear something crazy?" Jenna asked.

Amber and I looked at her.

"I've been thinking about asking Sara if Tank and I will get married."

"You want to marry him?" Amber asked.

Jenna lifted her shoulders. "I've thought about it."

"And what if Sara gives you a cryptic answer

like, 'Yes, you'll both get married'?" I asked.

Jenna scowled. "That's the only thing stopping me. I'd worry about whether that meant to each other or to someone else."

"You know, Jenna, it doesn't really matter what she sees. You have to decide what's best for you. Even though she saw things, we were the ones who made them happen," I said. "You were crazy about Tank before you saw the dragon. Amber's reasons for coming back had nothing to do with Sara's predictions. She came back because she wanted to do good things. Have some purpose. And I'm with Brady because I want to be. Not because he has a red hat."

"Are you saying we'd be where we are, even if we hadn't had a reading?" Jenna asked.

"Yeah, I think so. It was fun, but we didn't make any of our decisions because we thought we had to make what Sara saw happen. We determine our destinies."

"That is so corny," Jenna said. "As corny as what Tank said that first night. But I like it. I like it a lot."

I looked up and saw the guys walking toward us.

I grabbed Jenna's and Amber's hands and closed my eyes. "I see a night on Bourbon Street in our future."

They laughed.

"That was an easy prediction," Jenna said. "It's Friday night!"

We got up from the bench.

"We thought we'd head on over to Bourbon Street," Tank said when they got to us. "See what's happening there."

Jenna smiled. "We figured."

I kept myself nestled against Brady's side as we walked along the now-familiar street. We strolled slowly, listening to bands, watching the people, and celebrating the completion of the house.

"You know what you need?" Brady asked.

I laughed, because I knew where this was going. Sara had definitely rubbed off on me.

"Beads," he said.

He grabbed my hand, and I let him drag me farther into the craziness that's Bourbon Street.

Chapter 22

*I*t was our last night in New Orleans. We'd finished gutting another house and were halfway completed with its rebuilding. I wanted to stay and finish it, but we needed to get home, needed to start getting ready for school to begin. Another group of volunteers was going to finish the house. John said he'd let us know when the job was completed, in case we wanted to come back and welcome the family home.

I thought I probably would.

John and Sara had arranged for us to have an all-night party on a riverboat, their way of thanking us for the help we'd given them over the past six weeks. Even though none of us thought thanks were needed, we weren't going to say no to a party.

Brady and I were standing by the railing on the upper deck watching one of the paddle-wheels churn through the water of the Mississippi. There was a romantic element to it, but then, New Orleans is a city of romance. Since I'd been here, I'd come to appreciate what it had to offer: its history, its ghosts, its food, its music . . . its love of life.

Sometimes I think it takes almost losing something to realize how very precious it is.

Like what happened with Brady. I almost lost him. And in the losing, I'd finally discovered what I'd found. During the last few weeks, we'd grown closer, but I felt like I still had so much to tell him, so much he needed to know.

I needed—wanted—to tell him everything tonight, because tomorrow we'd be going our separate ways.

"Feeling better?" Brady asked.

We'd been down below with the other volunteers when I'd started to feel a little seasick. Who knew you could feel seasick on a river? But I guess moving on water is moving on water, regardless of what you call it. So we came up top. I was fine as long as I had plenty of fresh air to breathe. I guessed that was why the swamp hadn't bothered me. We hadn't been enclosed.

"Yeah, I'm okay now."

"Then let's go get something to eat," he said. "I'm starving."

He always was. Still, I nodded. The moment wasn't right for what I wanted to say. Or maybe a small part of me was still afraid— afraid of being hurt again.

But being hurt is part of life. And you learn to rebuild.

New Orleans had taught me that. I figured there would be other storms . . . more rebuilding. The city would shift, reshape, and change, but the heart of it would remain the same.

With Brady holding my hand, we walked past some benches and said hey to the volunteers who were sitting there. Then we went down the stairs that led into the dining room. Jenna, Tank, Amber, and Sean waved at us from a cloth-covered table near a window.

Jenna and Tank—they were tighter than

ever. Definitely in love. They were going to keep seeing each other when we got back to Houston. Jenna was going to apply to Rice, so she could go there next year after she graduated. And if Rice didn't accept her—it had pretty tough academic requirements—well, there was another university in Houston and there were community colleges. They'd find a way to be together. I had a feeling Tank was it for Jenna. The real deal. Forever.

I wasn't quite as sure about Amber and Sean, but then neither was she. She didn't know if he was the college love that Sara had predicted. What she did know was that meeting Sean had shown her that Chad wasn't the right one. And maybe Sean wasn't, either. Time would tell. But I had a feeling there was someone else in Amber's future.

After all, Sara had said Amber wouldn't find love this summer.

Not that I believe in all that mumbo jumbo.

Well, okay, maybe I did a little. It was hard not to after everything that had happened.

Even if I did believe we were in charge of our own destinies.

"Wow. They've got quite a spread," Brady said.

And they did. Red crawfish—piled high on a platter and on Brady's plate. Plus there was gumbo, étouffée, fried alligator, an assortment of shrimp and fish and chicken. I went with the fried shrimp and a bowl of étouffée.

We carried our plates and bowls over to the table where our friends were waiting.

"Sara's over there doing readings," Jenna said once Brady and I were settled. "Twenty dollars a pop. The money goes toward the rebuilding efforts."

I glanced over my shoulder. Sara was in a corner with a large window behind her. The sun was setting and the river visible through the window almost glowed red.

She was also holding Ms. Wynder's hand. I could see Sara talking, but of course she was too far away for me to hear what she was saying.

"Think she's telling her that curly red hair is a permanent part of her future?" Jenna asked.

Watching and grinning, John was sitting

beside Ms. Wynder. They were always together. Ms. Wynder had even stopped doing bed checks. I think maybe it was because she wasn't always back in the dorm on time to make them. Not that I was going to tell my mom that. She might not let me come back next summer if she thought there was "craziness" going on.

But then how could there not be? This was New Orleans.

"Maybe," I said.

"That wouldn't be much of a prediction," Amber said. "Ms. Wynder already told me that she's going to organize a group to come back over winter break."

"I think there is definitely something going on with those two," I said.

"That is just so . . . I don't know what it is." Jenna sighed. "But I just don't think of older people as falling in love."

"She's not that old," I said.

"Still. She's a . . . teacher."

I laughed. "Teachers fall in love. I think it's terrific. I just wish Sara had ended up with someone."

"Do you think she's seen him? Do you think

she knows who he is?" Jenna asked.

We all looked at Sean. He was the one who had spent the most time with her—before Amber had come back.

"What are you looking at?" he asked.

"Did she ever say anything? About her future, about her falling in love?" I asked.

He cracked open a crab claw. "She's married."

I was sure my eyes grew as wide as Amber's and Jenna's. "*What*? But you and she—"

"Friends. That's all. She's fun. Interesting."

"And her husband didn't mind?" Jenna asked.

"He's in the military, overseas." He held up a hand. "But she sees him on their porch, playing with a little boy, and they don't have kids yet, so—" He shrugged.

For the first time, I really, really, *really* hoped there *was* something to what she could see.

"So are we going to ask for another reading before we leave?" I asked.

"No way," Amber said.

"Uh-uh," Jenna emphasized. "From now

on life is a surprise."

"'A box of chocolates,'" Amber quoted. "It's the only way."

On the top deck, a small jazz band—friends of John's—was playing, and the music drifted down to us. It kept everything festive and fun. I was going to miss all this when we left.

I was going to miss Brady most of all.

We danced some, visited with the other volunteers, and said good-bye to the numerous friends we'd made. We all promised to keep in touch, but I didn't know if we would. Maybe at first. But then we'd all get busy. And we'd all just become memories.

That's what was going to happen with Brady.

It was our pact, our understanding, our agreement. We were together only as long as we were in New Orleans. And our time here was ticking away much faster than I wanted it to.

It was getting close to dawn as we stood on the top deck of the riverboat and watched the lights of New Orleans drift past. He'd had his arm around me a good part of the night.

But right now he was leaning forward, his

elbows on the railing, his hands clasped, as the riverboat began heading back to the dock.

"So . . . I guess this is it," he finally said. "The end of our arrangement."

"About that . . ."

He turned his head around and met my gaze . . . and waited.

And waited.

While I tried to figure out if I was willing to risk having my heart broken again. Because I'd fallen for him—hard. And it could break—easily. And this time, it would hurt worse than before. So much worse. Hard to imagine, but I knew it was true.

"I was wondering . . . ," I began.

"Yeah?"

"You were really patient with me in the beginning, when I was so guy shy."

He shrugged.

"Did the psychic see more than life is good?"

"Maybe."

"Tell me."

"What does it matter?"

"It doesn't. I'm just curious."

He sighed. "'I see life is good, but I see hurt. You're trying to rebuild something, but don't build too fast or it'll crumble.' So I decided to go slow."

"But you told me you didn't believe in psychic stuff."

"I don't. But when I met you, I thought, why risk it?"

So he'd gone slow, and been patient, and been understanding. Maybe he'd thought he was rebuilding a house.

But he'd rebuilt my heart.

And maybe I'd helped, just a little, to rebuild his.

"I want to keep seeing you," I blurted. "When we get home."

A slow smile eased across his face. "Okay."

That was all he said, but it was everything.

And then he was kissing me. And that was definitely *everything*. I wrapped my arms around his neck and pressed my body against his. It felt so right. It all felt so incredibly right.

Brady drew back, kissed my nose, my chin,

my forehead. Then he turned me around, put his arms around my waist, and held me close while we watched the sun easing over the horizon in the distance.

Sara had told me that she didn't see how things would end for us. But the truth was that she *had* seen the ending. It was the very first thing she'd seen when she took my hand.

With Brady kissing my neck, I watched as the last of Saraphina's predictions came true. That morning, the sunrise was indeed . . . spectacular.

It always is, when you're in love.

Author's Note

In June 2006, I went to New Orleans to sign books at the Romance Writers of America's exhibition booth at the American Library Association Conference. According to numerous newspaper reports, it was the first conference held in New Orleans following the devastation of Katrina. We were welcomed with open arms.

Friday night, my husband and I ate dinner at Bubba Gump's Shrimp Company. We were seated on the second floor. At another table was a large group of teenagers from out of town. They were laughing, cutting up, having a great time—after a long day of helping with the rebuilding efforts. While I didn't talk to them, after they left, our waiter explained who they were and what they were doing.

They served as the inspiration for this story.

—Rachel Hawthorne

Read on for a sneak peek at

Save the Date

by Tamara Summers

I'm never having a wedding.

When I meet my dream boy—who will not be (a) boring, (b) obnoxiously fit, (c) an enormous role-playing dork, or (d) a Taiwanese model I barely know, like certain other people's husbands I could mention—my plan is to skip the whole inevitable wedding catastrophe. Instead we'll do it the old-fashioned way. I'll club him on the head, drag him off to Vegas, and marry him in a classy Elvis chapel, like our caveman ancestors would have wanted.

None of my five older sisters will have to be bridesmaids. They won't even have to come if they don't want to, except Sofia, who will be my maid of honor. And I won't force her to wear the most hideous dress I can find, because I, unlike most of my sisters, am a kind and thoughtful person with, I might add, a terrific sense of style.

Don't get me wrong; I love my sisters. I'm the baby of the family, so they've always taken care of me and treated me like their favorite toy when we were growing up. In fact, they were always super-nice to me, until they turned into brides. So despite the bridesmaid dresses they have forced me to wear and the weirdos they've married, I do love them.

It's just not safe to get married in this family, at least not if I, Jakarta Finnegan, bring a date to the wedding, which presumably I will to my own wedding. This is because the Finnegan family suffers from a terrible Wedding Curse, or at least I do. I don't know what we did to deserve it.

I didn't figure this out until after Wedding #2. I thought all the insanity at my oldest sister's wedding (#1) was normal behind-the-scenes craziness. When the best man got stuck in a snowstorm in Indiana—in JUNE—I was like,

2

Huh, weird, and then when the organ player at the church came down with the mumps (in this century?), I thought it was strange, and sure, we were all a little freaked out by the flock of seagulls that crashed through the skylight in the reception hall during the cake cutting, but at no point did I think *Oops, my fault* or *Maybe I should uninvite Patrick to the wedding*. Afterwards, when this very first boyfriend I ever had broke up with me and fled in terror, it did cross my mind that maybe fourteen-year-old boys aren't cut out for nuptial ceremonies.

But it wasn't until the next wedding that alarm bells started to go off in my head. For instance, the day I asked my new boyfriend David to be my wedding date, the groom broke his wrist playing tennis and all three hundred invitations arrived back on our doorstep in a giant pile because they were missing two cents of postage. The day before the wedding, on the phone, was the first time I told David I loved him, and at that exact moment I got call waiting. When I switched over, it was one of my uncles hysterically calling to tell us that the hotel where all the guests were supposed to stay had burned down. And *then*, on the way to the wedding, when I kissed David in the limousine, *lightning* struck the car in front of us, causing a massive six-car pile-up in which no one was hurt, but everyone involved in the ceremony was an hour late.

Lightning. Mumps. And *seagulls*. I'm telling you, I'm not crazy. This is a very real curse. And that's not even getting into the emotional wreckage afterwards with David, but I don't like to talk about that.

So you can see why I'm not crazy about the idea of having a wedding myself. Besides, all the good ideas have been taken. There's nothing else I could possibly do that hasn't been done before. That's what happens when you have five older sisters.

My parents are the Ken and Kathy of the Ken and Kathy's Travel Guide series. They travel all the time, always to exotic, fabulous, far-flung locales, and their house is full of wild foreign art and knickknacks. But it's one thing to hang an African mask on your wall or put down a Peruvian llama rug. It's another thing alto-gether to name your children after the cities you've traveled to, don't you think?

Mine is by far the worst, of course. I mean, it figures; I'm the youngest, with five older sisters, so they had obviously run out of decent names for girls by the time I came along.

My sisters don't have it so bad: Alexandria, Sydney, Victoria, Paris, and Sofia. Those could totally be normal-person names, couldn't they? Not like Jakarta. I mean, seriously.

Alexandria, the oldest, is twenty-eight now. She's a lawyer, and she's tall and thin and blond and perfect-looking all the time. She got married two years ago, to another lawyer, Harvey the Boringest Man on Earth. That was the wedding with the snowstorm and the mumps and the sea-gulls. The one where Patrick broke up with me.

Then there's Sydney, who's a year and a half younger. She's athletic and short and full of energy, and she's a pediatrician. She married her tennis instructor a year ago. When I say "obnox-iously fit"? You have no idea. Marco makes me tired just looking at him. Even when he's sitting at our kitchen table reading the newspaper, you can tell he's burning major calories. Their wedding was the one where the hotel burned down and lightning hit a car and David was a majorly enormous jerk.

After Sydney came Victoria and Paris, only ten months apart and about as different as two people can be. Victoria, our "romantic" sister, is willowy and pale, wears her hair long and flowing like a nymph in a Pre-Raphaelite painting, and is very sweet and quiet . . . or, at least she was until she became a bride-to-be. Paris, on the other hand, has bright red hair cropped close to her head, a nose ring, and a burning desire to be the world's most famous female glassblower. My mom says she's "an individual."

Paris was enough to keep my parents busy for four years. Personally, if I had a daughter like Paris, I wouldn't ever have sex again, just in case there was another one like her lurking in there. The world couldn't SURVIVE two Parises.

Luckily, what they got instead was Sofia, my twenty-year-old sister who is also my best friend and the biggest genius in the universe. She's graduating from college this year—she triple-majored and still finished in three years.

Then there's me. Recently turned seventeen. I have normal curly brown hair, shoulder-length, and normal gray eyes.

I'm not blond or super-fit or perfect. Not romantic, not "an individual," and definitely not a genius. So what am I? I'll tell you what: a bridesmaid.

It feels like I've been a bridesmaid for three years straight, and we're not even halfway through my sisters yet. Victoria's wedding is this summer and then Paris . . . well, we'll get to that in a minute.

Read on for a sneak peek at

Picture Perfect

by Catherine Clark

"I can't *wait* to see all the guys."

You might have thought that was me talking, as I headed into the town of Kill Devil Hills, North Carolina, my destination for a two-week summer stay on the Outer Banks.

But no. It was my dad, of all people.

And it's not what you might be thinking *now*, either. He was talking about seeing his best friends from college.

We meet up every few years on a big reunion trip with "the guys," their wives, their kids, and other assorted members of their families. I think it's Dad's favorite vacation, because he and his buddies play golf, sit around reminiscing, and stay up late talking every night.

Even though that occasionally gets a little boring, I like going on these trips, because I've gotten to be friends with "the guys'" offspring: Heather Olsen, Adam Thompson, and Spencer Flanagan. It had been two years since the last vacation reunion for the four of us, which was *almost*, but not quite, long enough to make me forget what an idiot I'd made of myself the last time, when I was fifteen, Spencer was sixteen, and I'd told him that I thought he was really cool and that we really clicked and that I wished we lived closer because then we could . . . well, you get the gist. *Embarrassing*. With a capital *E*. Maybe three of them, in fact. EEEmbarrassing. Like an extra-wide foot that I'd stuck in my mouth.

But enough about me and my slipup.

We were getting close to the house number we were looking for when Mom shrieked, "Look! There's the house!"

My dad slammed on the brakes, which screeched like the sound of a hundred wailing—and possibly ill—seals. Dad has this awful habit of calling Rent-a-Rustbucket in order to save

2

money. Consequently, we end up driving broken-down automobiles whenever we go on vacation.

Dad backed up and turned into a small parking lot behind the tall, skinny house.

Ten minutes later, after dumping my suitcase in my room, I stood on the giant back deck, overlooking the ocean.

Down by the water, some kids were playing in the sand, building sand castles and moats, while others swam and tried to ride waves on boogie boards.

"I've made a list of top ten Outer Banks destinations. I read eight different guidebooks and compiled my own list," my mom was explaining to Mrs. Thompson when I walked over to them. "We'll need to go food shopping tonight, of course, and make a schedule for who cooks which night."

"Oh, relax, you can do the shopping tomorrow. Things are very casual around here," Mrs. Thompson said to her. She turned to me. "You should go say hi to Adam. He's down there, in the water."

"He is?"

She gestured for me to join her at the edge of the deck. "He's right there. Don't you see him?"

All I could see except for young kids was a man with large shoulders doing the crawl, his arms powerfully slicing through the water. "That?" I coughed. "That person is Adam?"

His stepmom nodded. "Of course."

Wow. Really? I wanted to say. When I focused on him again, as he strode out of the surf, I nearly dropped my camera over the railing and into the sand. "You know what? I think I *will* go say hi." *Hi, and who are you, and what have you done with my formerly semi-wimpy friend?*

I walked down the steps to the beach in disbelief. Last time I'd seen Adam, his voice was squeaking, and he was on the scrawny side—a wrestler at one of the lower weights, like 145. Not anymore. He had muscular arms and shoulders, and he looked about a foot taller than he had two years ago. His curly brown hair was cut short.

You look different, I wanted to say, but that would be dumb. *You look different and I sound like an idiot, so really, nothing's changed.*

Why was it that whenever I tried to talk to a guy, I started speaking a completely different language? Stupidese?

"Emily?" he asked.

I nodded, noticing that his voice was slightly deeper than I remembered it. It was sort of like he'd gone into a time machine and come out in the future, whereas I felt exactly the same. "Hi."

He leaned back into the surf to wet his hair. "You look different," he said when he stood up.

"Oh, yeah? I do?" *Different how?* I wanted to ask, but that was potentially embarrassing. Different in the way he did? Like . . . sexy? I waited for him to elaborate, but he didn't. "Well, uh, you do, too," I said.

"Right." He smiled, then picked up his towel and dried his hair. As he had the towel over his head, I took the opportunity to check him out again. Man. What a difference a couple years could make.